# HIGHLANDER UNDONE

*Highland Bound Series*

## ELIZA KNIGHT

# MORE BOOKS BY ELIZA KNIGHT

## PRINCE CHARLIE'S REBELS

*The Highlander Who Stole Christmas*

Prince Charlie's Angels

*The Rebel Wears Plaid*
*Truly Madly Plaid*
*You've Got Plaid*

## THE SUTHERLAND LEGACY

*The Highlander's Gift*
*The Highlander's Quest*
*The Highlander's Stolen Bride*
*The Highlander's Hellion*
*The Highlander's Secret Vow*
*The Highlander's Enchantment*

THE STOLEN BRIDE SERIES

*The Highlander's Temptation*
*The Highlander's Reward*
*The Highlander's Conquest*
*The Highlander's Lady*
*The Highlander's Warrior Bride*
*The Highlander's Triumph*
*The Highlander's Sin*
*Wild Highland Mistletoe (a Stolen Bride winter novella)*
*The Highlander's Charm (a Stolen Bride novella)*
*A Kilted Christmas Wish – a contemporary Holiday spin-off*
*The Highlander's Surrender*
*The Highlander's Dare*

THE CONQUERED BRIDE SERIES

*Conquered by the Highlander*
*Seduced by the Laird*
*Taken by the Highlander (a Conquered bride novella)*
*Claimed by the Warrior*
*Stolen by the Laird*
*Protected by the Laird (a Conquered bride novella)*
*Guarded by the Warrior*

THE MACDOUGALL LEGACY SERIES

*Laird of Shadows*
*Laird of Twilight*
*Laird of Darkness*

PIRATES OF BRITANNIA: DEVILS OF THE DEEP

*Savage of the Sea*
*The Sea Devil*
*A Pirate's Bounty*

THE THISTLES AND ROSES SERIES

*Promise of a Knight*
*Eternally Bound*
*Breath from the Sea*

THE HIGHLAND BOUND SERIES (EROTIC TIME-TRAVEL)

*Behind the Plaid*
*Bared to the Laird*
*Dark Side of the Laird*
*Highlander's Touch*
*Highlander Undone*
*Highlander Unraveled*

TOUCHSTONE NOVELLA SERIES

*Highland Steam*
*Highland Brawn*
*Highland Tryst*
*Highland Heat*

WICKED WOMEN

*Her Desperate Gamble*
*Seducing the Sheriff*
*Kiss Me, Cowboy*

❧

HISTORICAL FICTION

**Coming soon**!

*The Little Mayfair Bookshop*

TALES FROM THE TUDOR COURT

*My Lady Viper*
*Prisoner of the Queen*

ANCIENT HISTORICAL FICTION

*A Day of Fire: a novel of Pompeii*
*A Year of Ravens: a novel of Boudica's Rebellion*

FRENCH REVOLUTION

*Ribbons of Scarlet: a novel of the French Revolution*

# ABOUT THE BOOK

*Continue Ewan and Shona's tale... And find out what happened to Rory!*

With Logan and Emma away from the castle, Shona and Ewan are left in charge. The passion of their honeymoon is interrupted by an unexpected visitor seeking revenge on Rory MacLeod, who leaves them in desperate need to find the missing man. Unbeknownst to them, Rory has been transported to the future, where he is reunited with his long lost love, Moira, twin sister to Shona. Their attraction to each other still burns bright. As fate would have it, the four of them end up on a journey through the Highlands in an attempt to clear Rory's name, and solve the mystery behind Moira and Shona's birth. Passion. Love. Adventure. Danger. And a little bit of humor.

*For all of my wonderful readers. Every day I write is a joy because of you.*

# MOON MAGIC
## BY ELIZA KNIGHT

When thunder crashes
And lightning illuminates
Magic comes to pass.

Thistles sway, dancing
Purple petals and green stems
So very lovely.

Rain falls in crystal torrents
Sparkling drops on fingertips
Liquid Sustenance.

Black clouds shield the sun
Blanketing the world in darkness
Taking away our sight.

The castle climbs high
Battlements touching the sky
Striking fear below.

Warriors come now
Their weapons shined and sharpened
Prepared for vengeance.

We will survive this
Surge of ruthless cruelty
For we are strong, wise.

Loneliness touches
Us all and can break hearts
Leaving us wretched.

Massaging the soul
Flexing your capacity
To accept love's hold.

Flames burst, destroying
Everything in its path
Poisoning, tainted.

The evils of men
Devastate the innocent
Obliterating.

Do not surrender
To one who strips you, attempts
To watch you bleed dry.

Fear paralyzes
Only those who allow it
Be strong, be steady.

Afraid of being
Broken leaves one hopeless and

The future stark, bleak.

When hope does soar high
So too does joy and pleasure
Fostering courage.

Brave and courageous
Forge ahead, part from the past
And tumbling forward.

Beneath moon magic,
Lovers' gentle strokes bring bliss
And sweet surrender.

A precious ending
A love that shan't be broken
By the bonds of time.

## ❧ I ❧

### SHONA

*Scottish Highlands*
*Nearly spring, 1544*

Winter had been quiet. Too quiet.

Shona Fraser ran a finger over the frost-slickened stone outside of her bedchamber window, the crystals melting in the wake of her heated fingertip. Below, in the courtyard, the castle was slowly coming to life. The blacksmith and tanner, the armorer and the fletcher, all trudging toward their work huts, their footsteps leaving prints on the frosty ground. Servants stumbled their way toward the castle, their breaths puffing in clouds. Workers headed toward the fields to tend the thawing earth.

Spring was coming. The days were growing warmer. No longer was a fur-lined mantle required unless the sun had set.

A misty film covered the ground as the sun slowly burned off the remnants of frost. Within a few hours the rising sun would warm the air by twenty degrees or more.

Why, just yesterday, Shona had traipsed barefoot in her small medicinal herb garden, though not for too long.

"It's quiet," her husband Ewan said, coming up behind her. He pressed his lips to her bare shoulder, his hands sliding over her hips, settling into place.

Moments like this, tender and comforting, made her pause and give thanks. A slow smile crept on her lips as she leaned her head back onto his shoulder. She knew all too well that precious moments such as this could be shattered like a hammer hitting glass. "Our enemies have been hibernating just like the animals."

"Aye. With spring dawning, they will soon awaken."

Shona nodded, leaning her head back and reaching up to dredge her fingers in her husband's luscious hair. "But maybe we dinna have to awaken just yet."

Ewan pressed his hard cock to her bare buttocks. "Too late."

She giggled, turning in his arms to gaze into his crystal-blue eyes, as sparkling as the morning frost and as blue as a summer sky. Every time she looked at him he reminded her of a golden god. Hair the color of gold coins, with matching brows that slashed in arches on his broad forehead. Angled bone structure and a strong, chiseled jaw. His nose bore a distinct notch where it had been broken several times. A wide mouth with full lips that brought to mind every kiss they'd ever shared. "That makes two of us." Lifting up on her tiptoes she bit his chin and then pressed her lips to his. Soft warmth and delicious need.

No matter how many times she'd kissed him, every time felt fresh and delightful.

Ewan kissed her back, taking possession of what she offered. His hands cupped her face. His tongue delved to taste her mouth. His hard body melded to hers, warming her completely. She sighed with pleasure, her entire body coming alive, tingling. Her hardened nipples grazed his chest, her breasts felt heavy. Thighs quivered.

"My desire for ye never wanes," he murmured, sliding his lips over her throat, sucking at where her pulse beat.

Shona was going to answer, but the only sound that came out was a moan as his mouth clamped onto her nipple, sucking hard. Ewan growled, a primal sound that sent a shiver racing over her already tingling limbs. As though she weighed no more than a feather, he lifted her up. On instinct, she wrapped her legs around his hips, her arms around his neck. She gasped in shock and outrage when he sat her on the cold stone sill of the open window.

"Ewan!" She held onto him tighter.

"No one can see up here," he teased, his wiggling brows and crooked grin altogether wicked.

"If I can see down, they can most certainly see up." She peered over her shoulder, feeling heat rise to her face at the thought of the blacksmith viewing her bare arse as he pounded molten steel into some sort of weapon.

"Then they will see the captain of the guard taking a very naughty lass into custody. What shall your punishment be?"

Shona giggled and squirmed. "Take me down from here, else I arch my back in pleasure too much and fall out of the window."

"Och, I'd not thought of that." Ewan lifted her up. "Where else can I place this verra pretty arse?"

"How about the bed?" she asked, leaning forward to nip his ear and whisper, "I want to climb all over ye."

"Then that is the verra last place I shall put ye! For I am the conqueror this morn."

Shona laughed, and Ewan gently bit her shoulder as he twirled her around and finally settled himself on a chair with her straddling him. She shuddered at the delicious contact of his hard shaft slicking between her folds. Oh, how she wanted him inside her. She wiggled, the slight movement situating the head of his cock at her entrance.

Shona toyed with his hair and leaned close to whisper in his ear. "This was a bad choice for ye, captain." She flicked her tongue over his earlobe and then softly nibbled.

Ewan's breath was harsh against her neck, and when he spoke his voice had a gravelly edge. "Why is that?"

She shook her head. "Ye know verra well why." Shona reached between them, gripped his thick, pulsing cock and glided the head back and forth between her drenched folds.

Ewan groaned. "Och, I've now given ye the power."

"Will ye take it back?" she teased, her voice lowering, huskier, the power of how she could wield him in this position making her hotter. She continued to torment him—and herself, for every time the head of his cock slid against her nub of pleasure she jerked with need.

His hard shaft grew thicker in her grasp, and she grinned with knowing, as she slid her tongue over his neck, her teeth scraping on his Adam's apple.

"Oh, aye," he growled.

A wicked smile curved his mouth as he grabbed hold of her hips, shifted in the seat and then thrust upward. They both cried out at the invasion and the whip of erotic sensation lashing them both.

"Ye may be on top, but I've got the upper hand." His thumb grazed over her pleasure pearl and he bent forward to lick her nipple at the same time.

Shona gripped the back of his neck, her fingernails scratching upward, into his hair, and then she yanked. Hard. When he gave in, his head falling back, she playfully bit the sensitive spot at the crook of his neck, then licked and sucked where she'd wounded. Ewan drove his cock inside her ravenous body at the same time he landed a smack to her arse that cracked the air and left a pleasurable sting on her flesh.

This was a fun game they played. Push and pull. Power plays. Who was the conqueror? Who would surrender?

Three hard knocks on the door made them both stiffen. Shona glared down at her husband. But he held a finger to his lips and shook his head, then slowly continued to thrust upward, his cock filling her, his pelvis crushing to hers in shivery strokes.

Biting her lip to keep her cries of pleasure from escaping, her head fell back and for the moment, she allowed him to take over, but only for a moment. That was, until she realized she was completely without control and at his whim. Surrender inched closer.

Shona was going to let him win, because her body was wound taut, and pleasure radiated from every nerve. She wanted him. Needed this. Had to have it. Ewan grasped her chin, bringing her forward until their lips met, swallowing her cries as he continued to move inside her. He held tight to her hips, forcing her into a rocking rhythm in which he set the pace.

"Captain!" More knocks.

They ignored them. Their breathing hitched. Their pleasure growing to an intensity that left her gasping for air.

She was close to coming apart. Shona increased her pace, pushing against his grip on her hips, riding him as though her life depended on it. When the first tremblings of her climax began, she sucked on his lower lip. Ewan growled, thrusting harder, kissing her deeper to gulp her moans of gratification. The faster she moved, the harder he thrust, and then she was there, her body sparking, her insides quaking, pleasure bursting, limbs trembling, skin prickling. She cried out, and Ewan groaned beneath her, his own body shuddering and pulsing between her thighs.

Their movements slowed, bodies still quaking, heartbeats pounding, until she collapsed, her forehead falling to his, and she kissed him tenderly.

"Good morning, husband," she murmured against his lips.

"A verra good morning to ye, my wife."

"Cap-*tain*!" More banging.

Ewan sighed heavily, looking her in the eyes with irritation. "I suppose I ought to find out what the hell he wants."

"Aye, Lachlan's likely to have the guards break down the door if ye dinna answer it."

"He'd be forfeiting his life if he dared." Ewan kissed her once more. "Thank ye, love."

"For what?" she asked.

"For making every day of my life better."

Shona brushed the locks of hair that had fallen on his forehead back. "Ye have made my life infinitely better. Before ye, I wandered the woods of the Highlands, trying to figure out my purpose, what my fate would be, and the moment I saw ye, golden and glorious, I knew."

"Ye flatter me, my fiery maiden."

"I'm no maiden." She smirked.

"Ye're a nymph." He chuckled.

"Captain—I'm going to get the battering ram!" Lachlan called.

"For god's sake, man, have a care!" Ewan shouted.

Shona laughed at her husband's restraint from cursing. "I know what ye really wanted to say."

"I'll be saying it to him, too, when I'm on the other side of the door."

Ewan picked her up and tossed her onto the bed. "Stay put, woman. When I come back, I'm going to make love to ye properly."

Shona watched him dress, listening to him grumble the entire time, and then he kissed her one last time before he left, his angry insults in the hallway toward his lieutenant making her laugh. She hopped out of bed, tiptoeing on the chilled floor toward the water basin to wash up. From the sounds of things, though he promised to come back for another session of lovemaking, Lachlan was likely to keep him for a while. There was no need to wake the captain before he was on duty unless there was a problem.

Besides, there were a few things she needed to attend to before he returned. Duty beckoned.

## EWAN

"WHAT IN BLOODY HELL IS SO IMPORTANT?" EWAN growled at Lachlan.

Ewan had assessed the courtyard when he'd set his beautiful wife onto the windowsill and knew they weren't under attack, nor did there appear to be any other issues.

As soon as the snow and ice had thawed, their laird, Logan Grant, and Guardian of Scotland, and his lady wife, Emma, had ridden to Stirling Castle to pay homage to the infant queen who'd been crowned the previous fall. Mary Queen of Scots. The king was dead. Long live the queen.

Logan and Emma been unable to make the trek previously given the state of issues with the MacDonald's. Normally, Ewan was in charge of the guards and the castle's defenses, but with Logan gone for the time being, he was in charge of everything.

"Apologies, captain, but it was imperative I rouse ye." Lachlan sounded entirely too jovial about it.

"I was already roused," Ewan said through gritted teeth.

"More apologies then for... interrupting." Laughter echoed in his tone.

Ewan gritted his teeth and purposefully bumped Lachlan into the wall as they walked. "What is it?"

"A visitor's come." Lachlan righted himself, the smirk on his face damned irritating.

"Who?"

"The MacLeod."

"*The* MacLeod? Did he say why he was here?" They didn't have much contact with the young laird, only the warning that he and his clan wanted the wastrel Rory who'd been Shona's caretaker for years. But Rory had been missing for nearly three years. Shona didn't know where he was, nor did she seem to think he was as much a danger as Ranulf MacLeod said he was.

What to believe tore at Ewan. Of course he believed his wife, trusted her. And if the man had been so kind as to take her in when she was alone, and without coin, or knowledge of who she was, then he had to be a good person. But for a laird to warn them that Rory was a fugitive, to put a price on his head, well, that was a cause for concern that made Ewan's previous opinion waver slightly.

"He didna say, only that he needed to speak with ye."

"With me, or with the laird?"

"With ye."

Ewan nodded curtly, refusing to think anything more on it until he had all the facts. They entered into the laird's library where a lad, nay a man, Ewan supposed, though he couldn't be much out of his adolescence, stood.

"Ewan Fraser?"

"Aye." Ewan nodded to Lachlan who left the room, but would wait outside the door in case he was needed.

"Ranulf MacLeod. I've a need to speak with ye."

"I'm all ears, my laird. Can I have someone bring ye refreshment?"

MacLeod shook his head. "Let me get straight to the point. Ye're married to a woman named Shona, known to have harbored Rory MacLeod."

Ewan kept his emotions in check. "Shona is my wife. But ye've got the wrong of it. She did not harbor Rory, he took her in before he disappeared three years ago."

MacLeod continued as though Ewan had not spoken. "With your permission, I would like to question her."

Ewan crossed his arms over his chest, giving the young man a warning look. He might be a laird, be he was not on his own land. "What about?"

"Rory's whereabouts."

Ewan kept his voice cool. "She doesn't know."

"But, she might know something." Desperation echoed.

Ewan felt a twinge of pity for the young fool. "She doesn't." No way in hell was Ewan going to subject his wife to this young man's interrogation. "If ye have any questions ye'll have to ask me."

MacLeod puffed out his chest. "That bastard is responsible for my parents' deaths, as well as countless deaths within our clan. It is my right, by Highland law, that I should bring him to justice."

Ewan nodded curtly. "I agree. But I've never seen this man, and my wife's not had any knowledge of, or contact with him, in three years. He's disappeared. Might even be dead."

MacLeod's frown flattened into disappointment, even a hint of anxiety.

Ewan uncrossed his arms and blew out an annoyed breath. "Look, MacLeod, I'm not trying to hold back justice on a man who deserves punishment for his sins. If I see him, ye'll be the first one I contact. But I swear to ye, we've no knowledge of him at present."

MacLeod ran a shaky hand through his hair. "Its damned frustrating."

"I can understand that." Ewan went to the sideboard and poured himself a dram of morning whisky. He offered some to MacLeod who declined. "When did it happen, the murders?"

"Six years ago. I've been searching for the bastard for *six years*. He's like a ghost. One minute I spot him and the next, he just simply disappears. We'd thought he was hiding out in a cottage in the woods, close to this castle, but it was abandoned. I canna sleep. I can barely eat."

Ewan poured another round and this time MacLeod asked for one. "That's the last place we saw him."

"Thanks," MacLeod said, taking the offered drink. "The clan elders are encouraging me to let it go. But I canna. Rory's betrayal left our clan helpless."

MacLeod didn't look like much a trailblazer. Likely his clan elders did most of the leading.

"Ye were just a lad when ye took your father's place?"

"Aye."

"Look, I'm no chief, but there is one thing I've learned being in a position of leadership."

MacLeod sipped his whisky, watching Ewan intently.

"Ye canna let revenge lead your life. Ye canna let it rule your mind, chart the course of your actions, or the leadership within your clan. Ye must eat. Ye must learn to settle your mind in order to sleep. I hate to say it, but your elders are probably right. And ye know what?" Ewan tried to offer a smile of encouragement. "Most times, the thing ye've been searching so hard for, it presents itself as soon as ye stop looking."

"So ye think I should quit?" The furrowed brow returned.

"Nay, I didna say quit. I think ye should rest a spell. Concentrate on your clan, show them ye're willing to work with them and help them grow. Be a leader. Honor your parents. Rory cannot hide forever."

MacLeod tossed back the rest of his whisky. "All right. But if ye see him, hear of him, ye'll send word right away?"

"Aye. And I'll be certain to let my chief know when he returns, in case he saw the man on his travels."

"I thank ye, Captain Fraser."

Ewan set their glasses back on the sideboard. "I'm sorry that tragedy has touched your family."

"Seems inevitable, does it not? I know not one person who has not experienced tragedy."

That sort of wisdom in a man so young had to mean there was hope for him yet. "Aye, this is true."

Ewan thought of Shona, waiting for him upstairs. How much had she endured? She didn't even remember all of it, but it must have been dreadful if her mind wanted to keep it from her.

"I'll have the kitchen pack a few provisions for your return journey," Ewan said.

MacLeod waved his hand in denial. "That will not be necessary. I should journey back to Skye right away. I've been gone long enough now."

Ewan reached out to shake MacLeod's arm. He was little more than a lad, and Ewan felt slightly sorry for him.

"Good luck, MacLeod."

"My thanks. For more than just agreeing to look for any sign of Rory, but for what ye said. It's high time I stepped into my father's boots."

And then the lad was gone and Ewan was left staring out of the library window toward the loch beyond. Rory would not have been the first man to simply disappear. If a man was skilled enough, he could live a life in the shadows for decades.

Ewan had been unable to brush off the haunting shadow of his wife's companion and protector from the moment he'd met her all the way until today, and he was afraid he never would. He owed Rory his thanks for having kept Shona safe for all those years, but he also wanted answers. Ewan just couldn't believe that Rory was as evil as MacLeod thought he was, but neither could he disbelieve MacLeod who seemed genuinely disturbed.

From what Ewan understood, the young laird had not been with his parents when they'd been murdered. The clan elders had swept him to safety when the siege broke out. Rory had been a captain of the guard, just like Ewan himself.

What would make a captain turn on his laird and mistress?

There was nothing that would make Ewan turn on Logan and Emma. He simply couldn't. That meant Rory had to have some of the answers. Answers none of them may ever get if he simply vanished into the ether.

Ewan watched the ripples on the surface of the loch below. For as long as he could remember, he'd loved to watch the ripples. There was always the hope that Nessie would show her beautiful, sleek head. He remembered being a young lad, several years younger than MacLeod and swearing he'd seen the long neck rise from the depth of the loch. He couldn't remember much else from his youth. His earliest memories were waking in the loch, scrambling with the water for his life. He'd managed to swim to the edge, grab hold of tree roots and hoist himself, battered and drained, from the water. Once on land, he'd passed out, was rescued by crofters, only to be woken by Logan's face peering down into his when they brought him to the castle. Logan had insisted that Ewan remain with him. Ewan's laird was his savior, his dearest friend and family. Granted, not all captains had a relationship as close with their laird as Ewan had with his, but he'd never met one who wouldn't have laid down his life for his leader. Not one.

That was why Ewan couldn't let this go. There had to be more to the story. More to what happened out on the marsh when the Laird and Lady of MacLeod were butchered. If anything, Ewan owed it to his wife to try and find the answers.

"Where are ye Rory MacLeod?"

## 🦋 2 🦋

SHONA

"Who is that?" Shona asked one of the other maids as they exited from the granary where they'd been gathering supplies.

As predicted the sun had warmed the air tremendously, and she breathed in the scent of peat and the crispness of coming spring. No longer would she fear frostbite as she worked.

"I think that's MacLeod."

Shona's stomach flipped, and air gushed from her lungs so quickly, she coughed. "*Laird* MacLeod?"

"Aye." The lass shrugged. "I heard someone say it."

Shona ignored the perplexing stare from the other servant and worked to smile, though it felt forced. She ducked her head, sifting in her basket of herbs. "Oh, I forgot something," she muttered, stepping back into the granary, not checking to see if the lass believed her lie.

The maid called goodbye and sauntered off. As soon as she was out of sight, Shona crept back to the opening to peer out at the retreating figure of Laird MacLeod. His swagger, the hair on his head, the angles of his face—they were all painfully familiar. Did all the MacLeods look alike? If not for his smaller stature and age, she might have mistaken him for Rory. What could he have been doing here? Was he still searching for Rory? She knew they said he'd done terrible things, but she didn't believe any of the rumors. Not one.

Aye, she'd only known Rory a few years, since she'd lost her memory; the only times she could recollect were with him. He'd taught her so much, protected her. He'd been her only friend, and like a brother. When he'd disappeared, she'd searched for him day in and day out for two years. And then she'd met Ewan. When Ewan had wanted her to come back to Gealach with him she'd been hesitant to leave the cottage in case Rory came back. That was a year ago, and she'd kept her eye for him since, but there had been nothing. As though he simply vanished from the earth.

And now his laird was looking for him. Again. What was the renewed search for? Had he been spotted?

Rory had never told her exactly what happened to separate him from his previous life, mostly that something awful occurred and that he'd been thrust into another territory. That he'd been a coward, and because of that, he had pledged his life to solitude and reflection. Until he found her. That was when he'd pledged himself as her protector. Perhaps a way of making amends with whatever demons tormented his conscience.

Shona never really understood all of what he said. He'd been forced to leave his clan. There were plenty of people ousted by their clan. She'd always assumed he must have slept with the laird's wife. A scandal. Made sense since he never tried to woo her or any other lass. But, the laird, he was so young. That couldn't have been it.

Then there were the awful things that Ewan had accused Rory of the year before. Well, actually, it had been Ewan's laird—her laird—Logan, that had shared the accusations of Laird MacLeod.

Murder. Betrayal.

Rory was no outlaw, even if he'd been forced to live like one. She knew, in her soul, that he was innocent of their accusations. But her beliefs would never be a good enough reason to acquit him.

Tightening her hold on the basket of herbs, she'd gathered from their drying place in the granary, she rushed back to the chamber she shared with Ewan. There was an adjoining room that she'd changed into a workroom where she could create various tinctures and ointments for those in need. Being named the clan healer had been a dream come true—except for the occasional accusation of witchcraft. That was not fun at all.

A long, wooden worktable graced the center of the room, on which she placed her basket of herbs. There were shelves in front of her and shelves behind. On the shelf behind her were all the ingredients and tools she needed for her trade, and on the shelves in front were the pre-made vials, each wrapped in a slim piece of parchment that was connected at the back with wax, and then labeled with ink. *Headache. Fever. Dysentery. Nausea. Nerves. Sleep. Burns. Cuts. Stitches.* All sorts of healing tinctures, ointments and salves.

Beneath the high table, was a shelf, which held her three medical bags. She'd sewn the leather satchels herself and each had a different colored wool handle so she knew which to grab if it were an emergency. Red for battle. Blue for childbearing. Green for illness.

There were no windows in the room, so, she lit several candles until she felt there was enough light from which to work by.

While she was waiting for Ewan to return, there was a particular ointment that Emma had asked for, as well as the tincture for the butcher's ague, and an herbal remedy she wanted to give Ewan to help with his night terrors. Her poor husband was still waking up in the middle of the night covered in sweat, his heart racing and fear in his eyes. There was much he'd had to endure; the man had nearly died at least twice in the last six years. If there was anyway she could make him feel better, then she needed to try.

There was a soft knock on the workroom door, and faint as it may have been, it startled Shona, making her clink her vials and bowls together, nearly dropping two.

"Come in," she called, righting the containers, and sending up a prayer of thanks that all damage had been avoided.

Ewan opened the door, filling the expanse with his broad, muscled body. The candlelight flickered over his tan face and flaxen hair, making him look like a mirage. "I'm sorry it took longer than I expected."

Shona smiled indulgently. "I would wait forever for ye."

Ewan covered the few feet of distance between them in a single stride, tugging her into his arms and planting a kiss on her mouth. She sighed against him, leisurely wrapping her arms around his waist.

"Ye're too good for me," he murmured.

"Never. We are a perfect pair." She meant the words whole-heartedly, but that didn't stop the nervous thump of her heart against her ribs. Had he come to tell her about MacLeod? How much danger was Rory in?

Ewan held her at arm's length, gazing at her for a long moment before he spoke. "We had a visitor."

She swallowed down her nerves. "I saw."

"I gather ye know it was MacLeod." Keeping one hand on her hip, Ewan picked up one of her vials with the other, examining the dark green contents, perhaps in an attempt to distract her from their conversation.

Distraction wouldn't work.

She softly disengaged herself and took the vial, setting it right where she'd had it. "Was he here for Logan?"

*Please say aye.*

"Nay, love."

"Ye?"

*Please say aye.*

"Nay. He was looking for ye."

"Me?" She somehow managed to keep the shock from her voice, a task that took all the effort she had, which left little for her trembling hands. She let go of the clinking vials. "What did he want with me?"

"Answers."

"Answers to what?" She asked the question even though she had an idea of what the answer would be.

"Rory."

Her heart sank. There had still been a little part of her that hoped Rory had nothing to do with it. "And what did ye tell him?"

"That ye had no answers to give."

Relief made her shoulders sag. "I do not have any."

Ewan touched her chin, gently coaxing her to meet his gaze. "Have ye told me everything ye know?"

She glimpsed the question in his eyes. "Do ye not trust me?"

"I trust ye. Ye know that. But please, just answer me. Is there something else?"

She shook her head, turning to her worktable and shaking one of the vials to mix the contents.

Aye, there was something else, but nothing to do with Rory. She was not yet ready to share with him the secret she'd been holding onto for awhile now. The secret she and Emma had divulged to each other—that she was not from this time. She couldn't tell him until she knew for certain. She didn't even know what time she was *from*. A small part of her was beginning to suspect that Rory would not be found by anyone because he wasn't here anymore to be discovered. She also couldn't tell Ewan that her pull to the moon had been getting stronger with each passing night. Memory after memory came tunneling back stronger than before: the strange woman in her visions—*herself*—reading a book and drinking a glass of wine; standing on a boat with thick sails and breathing in the salted air; riding on a large, fast-moving, overlong, iron wagon full of people; frantically scribbling in a journal; and one thing she was familiar with—picking herbs. Except the other woman picked herbs in an unnaturally lit, domed building, with strange whirring noises, and odd boxy objects. And there was someone else there. Someone who looked just like her, but with darker hair. And they smiled and laughed a lot. This alternate world that haunted her. The memories that seemed so real, she could almost reach out and grab hold of them.

Nay, these were confessions that served her better if they remained hidden in her mind.

And there was more. She feared tonight the most, when the moon would be full, for if that far off world could come to her so strongly from the moon's pull when it was only a crescent, what would happen with the full power of its silver body? Unless, she was distracted by it. Using its power for some other desire greater than figuring out her past?

"There is nothing else," she lied. Then turned to him with a wild, wanton wiggle of her brows and curl to her lips, hoping to change the subject. "But there is something I *was* wondering about."

"Aye?"

"We've been trying..." They'd been trying for months to conceive a child.

"Aye...?"

"There is a tale amongst the clanswomen that if we make love by the sacred stone, in the glen that sits on the rise beyond the loch, the night of a full moon that we will conceive. Tonight is a full moon."

Ewan circled her waist with his arms and kissed the side of her neck. "Then let us go there."

"Are ye certain?" She couldn't help the thrill that filled her voice. She desperately wanted a child, and though Emma had yet to tell Logan about their own conception, she did tell Shona that the old tale of making love by the stone worked for her. This was the perfect distraction from her past—creating a future.

"Of course," he said, pressing his lips to hers for another heated embrace.

Lord, but she loved her husband. Just when she was breathless and ready to demand he make love to her, he slowly drew away.

He tapped her on the tip of her nose, a satisfied smile on his ruggedly handsome face. He loved to rile her up, make her pant with need. A delicious torment she'd remember the rest of the day until she got him alone again.

"I will let ye finish your remedies, while I see to the castle's defenses. We will sneak out to the glen this afternoon, afore the sun sets."

"I will have Cook pack us a picnic."

Ewan shook his head. "Nay, love. I'll slip into the kitchen and gather it myself without anyone the wiser. I dinna want to be followed under pretense of protection, else we make a show for them all." He gave her behind a little pinch.

Shona yelped, and slapped playfully at his roving hand. "For a man who used to love a show at Hildie's Tavern, ye've become quite the prude."

That had her husband lunging for her, lifting her up into the air and settling her rear on the worktable, his hips spreading her thighs. "Prude, eh?" He bent forward and bit her nipple through her dress, his hard cock grinding against the apex of her thighs.

Tremors of need coursed through her, and she gripped the back of his shirt, prepared to yank it free from his belt. Shona gasped in pleasure. "Mercy! I surrender."

"'Tis not mercy I shall give." He tugged a little harder on her nipple. "Only pleasure."

But a knock at the door stopped his delicious torment. "Mistress?" a woman called from the other side. "Have ye the tincture for the butcher? His wife begs ye hurry."

Ewan gave her one last longing look and then set her down on the floor with a smack to her bottom. "Your patients await."

"I'll see you when the sun is near setting."

"Aye. Be ready, for I will show ye just what a prude I am not."

Shona giggled. "I'll be counting on it."

As soon as her husband slipped from the workroom back into their chamber, she called out to the servant, "Just a moment," then straightened her skirt and hair.

When she answered the door, the butcher's wife was waiting beside the servant in the corridor. The poor woman was ringing her hands.

"Please, mistress, he's gotten worse overnight. He's sweating something fierce and tossing and turning."

"Sounds like his fever is breaking, madam." Shona ushered the woman over to the worktable and reached for the vial filled with an herbal tincture. "This will help. And plenty of bone broth. Chamomile boiled in water, too."

"Thank ye so much. We're so blessed to have the Lady of the Wood among us."

Shona smiled, hiding how she really felt about the

moniker. "Ye're verra welcome. Do keep me informed of his progress and if ye need more tincture."

"I will, mistress."

When the butcher's wife had left, Shona finished up the rest of her concoctions, slipping another special oil she'd been testing into the pouch tied to her belt.

Shona ventured down to the kitchen next, a usual part of her day, to see if Cook had any food that needed to be delivered to the ill folks in town. The laird of Gealach was ever generous and took care of his people. If they could not feed themselves, he made sure they and their families did not starve. This was a notion Shona really took pleasure in seeing done. It also helped her to get to know the people and examine her patients at the same time.

The rest of the day passed quickly. She watched eagerly as the sun rose high into the sky and then began to make its descent. Sunrise would be in a little over an hour.

With hurried steps, she made her way back to her chamber to wash up and gather several plaid blankets. Though winter was leaving them, the air was still crisp. She'd slept under a blanket of stars several times with her husband. They'd not be cold. He was as warm as a fire, and with blankets to boot; they'd be mighty cozy. Besides, if the rumors were true, the magic of the glen would keep them safe from cold.

As she finished preparing, Ewan slipped into their chamber with a big smile on his face and a satchel over his shoulder.

"Are ye ready, *mo chridhe?*"

"Aye!" She rushed him, throwing her arms around his neck. "This is going to be exciting."

He kissed her soundly. "I canna wait to undress ye in the glen before the sun sets so I can see the light of gloaming kiss your skin."

"And I want to lay ye down on the grass and ride ye as nature intended."

Ewan chuckled, giving her rear a slap. "Ye're a naughty wife."

She walked her fingers from his chest to his belt buckle. "And ye'd have me no other way."

"That is the truth." He made a sound of approval. "I'd not be able to survive with a curmudgeon as a wife."

Shona picked up the satchel she'd packed and handed it to her husband. "Lucky it is ye got me, because I've a feeling Hildie would definitely be a killjoy."

That made Ewan howl with laughter, since Hildie— Ewan's longtime mistress—would have been anything but. Madam to the most infamous brothel in Grant lands, Hildie made Shona look like a nun.

"Och, but ye do make me laugh, wife."

Shona peered behind her through the narrow window. "Are ye ready to escape? If we do not hurry, we will not make it before the sun sets."

Already, her body was vibrating with anticipation.

## 3

### SHONA

They made it to the top of the mountain just as pink and orange ribbons fringed the horizon. Despite the inclined elevation, the air was warmer, edging more toward summer than spring. Shona smiled, excitement vibrating through her veins.

"This is beautiful," she said, gazing at the glen where wildflowers seemed to bloom more readily than they did below on the moors. A vibrant blanket of red, yellow, purple and white. The trees swayed gently with the breeze, and a beam of light from the setting sun glowed in sparkling rays onto the single stone, twice as tall as a man and three times as wide, that graced the center of the clearing.

"This place feels magical." Ewan dropped their satchels in the center of the clearing, turning in a circle. "I've only ever been here a few times afore, not to stay, and I never noticed."

"It does," Shona whispered, suddenly frightened of her plan. The enchanting whimsy of the glen left her feeling light and carefree. Was its magic already working? And to what end? *I want to stay. I want a child.*

She'd wanted to come to the top of the glen in hopes that

the magic of this place would help them to conceive, but now she had fears of perhaps a different sort of magic. The sort that would take her back to wherever she'd come from, forever separating her from Ewan. *I want to stay. I want a child.* She continued to repeat the words in her mind, hoping Fate would be swayed.

"Maybe we should—" she started.

Ewan must have sensed her hesitation. His fingers laced with hers and he tugged her toward the stone. "We should stay."

"But—"

"Whatever happens was meant to be. We want to start a family, no?"

"Aye. We do."

"Then perhaps the stone's magic will bless us." Ewan pressed his hand flat to the center of the stone. "Touch it."

Shona place her hand beside Ewan's, feeling the stone warm at her touch.

"Oh, merciful stone," Ewan murmured. "Bless us. Bless our union. Lead us to the path that is right for us, for we wish to bring another into this world."

Shona's eyes widened, and she added, "A child of our own, that we two have created," just in case the stone got confused and thought they wanted to bring forth another time-traveler instead.

"A child of our own," Ewan said beaming a smile at her.

Shona couldn't help but smile back. Her husband was a contagious man when it came to his moods, and she often found herself mirroring his joy and even his sorrow.

Ewan shifted behind her, covering both of her hands on the stone with his own. He kissed the side of her neck and whispered, "I'm going to make love to you first standing right here, touching this magical rock."

Shona shivered, her nipples tightening, her core growing

slick. "I love ye," she murmured. "I never want to be without ye."

"And ye never shall, *mo chridhe*." His mouth skimmed the line of her neck, shivers following the path he created.

Shona's head fell back, resting on his strong shoulder, her mouth opened in a sigh. She closed her eyes, relishing the feel of his hands roving over her ribs, cupping her breasts, his teeth tugging at the collar of her gown, his steely erection pressed taut to her buttocks. Her hips tilted back, a silent invitation, nay, a pleading, for more of his ardent caresses.

"Shona," he whispered, fingers slowly inching her gown up over her thighs, exposing her naked flesh to the glen, the sun and the moon.

Firm, hot fingers slid beneath the globes of her rear, massaging, pulling her firmer against his arousal. Her breaths came quick, harsh and her heart echoed in the gentle breeze.

"Take me," she begged.

A coarse palm skated over her naked hip, to the curls damp with her desire. Fingers parted her folds to tease the knot of flesh that pulsed, and behind her, he gripped his cock sliding it deliciously along her wet entrance.

"Please," she pleaded.

"I love the way ye respond," he growled, biting her earlobe with just enough force that a tiny itch of pain melded with the intense pleasure of his mouth on her skin. "Your cunny is wet... hot... and ready for me."

She trembled, her core tightening into what felt like a hundred coils ready to burst. Shona arched her back, pressing her naked buttocks harder against him, demanding he enter her.

"Ye want me, say it," he commanded.

"I want ye, husband. Now."

"Tell me what ye want me to do."

Saints, but his voice... So rugged. So deep. So demanding. "I want ye to make love to me."

"Tell me how."

His fingers worked magic, sliding in a soft circular pattern over her sex, making her knees weak, and she was finding it difficult to answer. To think. To breathe. Only to feel. "I want ye to thrust inside me. Hard. And harder." She licked her lips. "I want ye to make me come."

"Oh, aye, I'm going to make ye come, love."

He ceased gliding is cock between her folds, notching it at her entrance, and arcing up, and thrusting deep inside her.

Shona let out a breath she didn't know she was holding, her back arching. If he'd not been holding her up, if she didn't have the stone as a sturdy hold at her front, she'd have surely collapsed from pleasure.

Gradually, he pulled out, plunging hard again. His fingers continued their torment, slow then fast, while behind her, his pace brought her just to the brink, before he'd stop and leisurely glide in and out of her tightened channel.

"How does this feel?" Ewan asked.

"So... good," she croaked.

"Show me how good."

Her fingers tightened against the stone, nails digging into the marble surface, as he relentlessly thrust inside of her, continued to stroke her nub, until streaks of light shown behind her eyes. Shona's eyes popped open. She watched the sun slide just under the horizon while the moon made its silvery light known, appearing to spark and wink at her conspiratorially. At that very same moment, her body quickened. Pleasure radiated from every inch. Intense in its pulsations. Her limbs shook. She cried out, feral and primal, like a howl toward the moon.

But her husband was not done with her. He did not allow himself to finish. Instead, he withdrew from her body, and whipped her around, pressing her back to the stone as his mouth claimed hers, a hand on her hip, the other threading into her hair at the nape of her neck.

"God, I love ye," he was saying as he kissed her.

She clung to him, kissing him back hungrily, until she remembered what she'd put into her pouch.

"I brought ye something," Shona whispered, urgent.

"Show me."

She bent to her satchel, pulled the oil from her pouch, and then poured a few drops onto her hand.

"What is it?"

"Ye'll see." Shona slipped her hand beneath his plaid, palming his thick cock and gliding the mint-herbal oil over his flesh.

Ewan's mouth fell open and he gasped as curse. "*Mo chreach.*"

"Aye." The oil would make his skin tingle, make his climax longer, increase his stamina, create more seed, and allow for a very fast recovery time so they could make love for hours and hours both of them climaxing as many times as they wanted to. "'Twill help with both pleasure and conception."

He cursed again in Gaelic, his eyes hooded with desire as she worked his length with her hand.

Shona stepped up on tiptoe, capturing his mouth as he had laid claim to hers. "Ye're mine," she whispered.

"Always."

As she kissed him, she continued to pump her hand up and down his rigid cock, feeling him grow in size, fuller, stiffer. Her own sex twinged; wet need dripping down her thighs. She'd never get over how much she wanted him. How much her body needed him. Ewan tugged at the laces of her gown, the fabric falling to her feet, and then he was working on removing her chemise. Their lips parted only as he pulled it over her head.

Shona stood nude before him, his weighty cock in her hand. "Let me not be the only one so thoroughly naked." She smiled wickedly, but before he could undress, she dropped to her knees, unable to get the idea of his cock in her mouth out of her mind.

Keeping her hand around the root, she slid her tongue over his firm, plush head, tasting the mint and oils, feeling them tingle on her tongue.

"Fuck me," Ewan groaned. "The heat. The cold. 'Tis..." But his voice broke off on a moan as she sucked him in deep.

Shona loved his cock. Loved the feel of it on her tongue. The thickness of it stretching her mouth. The heat of it pulsing between her lips. Up and down she went, pumping her hand in the opposite direction of her mouth, meeting in the middle and then back. She would have kept going, would have gone until his seed poured down her throat, but that was not how a child was conceived, so when Ewan gripped her hair and tugged her up, she obeyed his silent command.

He stripped himself naked, and lifted her in the air, only to settle her rapidly onto his discarded plaid. "More oil."

He stood above her, his cock proudly looming at attention. 'Twas hard not to rise up on her knees once more to taste his skin, to hold the power of his mighty length in her mouth—and be the one in charge.

She reached for the vial, pouring another healthy amount onto her palm and stroked him until he groaned for mercy, his head falling back.

"Good God, what is in that?"

"My secret recipe."

"I'll never last," he said, his voice husky.

"Oh, aye, but ye will." She couldn't help her grin. What power she held with just a few strokes of her hand.

Ewan dropped to his knees and she shoved him backward,

climbing over his thighs and straddling his hips, his turgid flesh resting against her curls and touching her belly.

"Ye're a beautiful vixen." His grin was wicked, delicious.

Shona leaned over him and sucked on his lower lip. "And ye're a wicked Highlander."

"No doubt." He gripped her hips and lifted her enough for his cock to slide along the wetness of her nether-lips, and when he reached the rim of her opening, he thrust upward.

They both cried out at the breathtaking invasion. The connection of heated flesh on heated flesh. The blazing inferno of desire, need, and magic. For there was magic here. There was magic within them. Whenever they were together the world seemed all the better, all the more amazing and wondrous.

Without waiting for his cue, she began to swivel her hips back and forth, delighting in the rippling sensations of pleasure the movement elicited. She arched her back, gyrating to a rhythm that seemed to vibrate in the very air.

Ewan grabbed hold of her hips, trying to slow her down, but she couldn't. The oil on his cock made the sensations around her folds and inside of her slick channel sing with tingly pleasure. She rode him quicker, bouncing on his hips as though she'd drive him through the ground. And then, she was breaking apart, her climax sharp and sweet. Ewan dug his fingers into her hips, shuddering beneath her.

"Saints..." he growled, the power of his seed shooting hot.

"Ye're not done," she teased.

"Nay." The moon shone on his face revealing his wonder. "How is this possible? I'm still hard as stone."

"'Tis the oil, and it's working just as I hoped it would."

"I'll never leave your bed again, woman."

Shona laughed, her hands flattened to his chest as she dragged in a recovering breath. "At least not for tonight." A breath later, she started to move again, surprised at how much stamina they both appeared to still have. She wanted more, so much more. And just the thought of that, of her husband, of their love, of this moment, and she was riding him hard once more.

"I love your skin," Ewan murmured, his hands stroking upward when he realized she'd not relent on her pace. He cupped her breasts, leaned up on his elbow to take a nipple into his mouth. "I love your scent. Your taste."

She groaned, her movements faltering at his touch. That was his game, to distract her. And he won. Ewan flipped her over onto her back, his cock still buried deep inside her.

With tortured slowness, he withdrew from her body. "I love the way ye feel wrapped around my cock." Then thrust back in. "I love the way your eyes roll back when I do this." Again, slow withdraw, hard thrust. "I love the way your lips look plump and rosy when I kiss ye." And he lowered himself, capturing her mouth with demanding fierceness. "I love the way your legs wrap tight around my hips so I can thrust harder, deeper." And he did.

Stronger. Wilder.

Spine-tingling. Earth-shattering.

Stunning. Exquisite.

He moved within her, over her, all around her, until she could barely breathe, couldn't think at all, and was once more crying out, her nails scaling down his back, his answering moan an echo on the wind.

But Ewan wasn't done with her yet.

"Ballocks," he cursed. "I want ye again."

"Dinna stop," she moaned, her body on fire with need and potent desire.

Once more, he flipped her over, onto her belly this time, impaling her still quaking core. He rode her from behind, until they were both slickened with sweat, shaking and crying out in climaxes that rivaled all others.

They collapsed onto the plaid. The moon was out in full, shining its silver light onto them. Shona curled up beside him, savoring his arm around her. Resting her head on his shoulder, she traced circles on his chest while he lazily drew lines up and down her back.

"The moon looks bigger up here," Shona murmured.

Ewan glanced down at her. "Aye. It's shining off your slick skin."

She giggled, when he tickled her ribs, warm and satiated.

"Are ye hungry?" Ewan asked. "I packed us a meal."

"Famished."

He covered her with one of the plaid blankets and she snuggled into it when he rose to grab the satchel of food he'd brought with him.

"Wine," he said, pulling out a corked jug. "Bread. Cheese. And meat." He presented before her, a loaf of bread, large hunk of cheese and an entire roasted duck. "A meal fit for my wife."

Her mouth watered. "Ye spoil me."

"But I'm not quite done. Dessert." He pulled out an entire cake. "An almond cake with golden raisins baked in."

"Oh, Cook is going to be mad when she sees that gone." Shona smiled with glee, like a child who'd snuck a whole army's worth of treats.

Ewan wiggled his brows. "Likely. Shall we have dessert first?"

"I feel like we already did," Shona giggled.

"That is true. And perhaps, I want more dessert before the night is through."

"I would be more than happy to give it to ye."

They ate, chatting about the castle, Emma and Logan, and then as Shona took a nice, large sip of wine, Ewan said, "We need to find Rory."

"Rory?" She was sort of hoping they'd not talk about him again, at least not tonight.

"Aye."

"Why?" The wine soured in her belly.

"Because, love, I'm afraid he's in danger."

"From who? 'Tis MacLeod, isn't it?"

"Aye. He's got half the Highlands searching for Rory. I convinced the lad to go home, to concentrate on his clan and duties, but his parents' death will haunt him forever if he does not gain some closure. I'm certain he'll return to his search afore long."

Her face fell and she stared into the opening of the wine jug. "But he didn't do anything wrong."

"I know ye believe that, love, and I'm inclined to agree. But the lad was adamant that Rory murdered his parents and is responsible for the deaths of many in his clan."

"I just can't believe it. Rory is kind and gentle. He took me in when he didn't have to. I wasn't a prisoner, or his slave. He was my friend. He *is* my friend."

"That is why we must find him first."

Shona shook her head. "I've searched everywhere I could think of."

"I believe ye did, lass, but maybe there is one clue we haven't unturned yet."

"Like what?" She took another sip and then passed him the jug, unwilling to mention the one thing she thought might have happened to Rory—time travel.

"I'm not certain of it yet, but maybe if we talk about him, if ye show me your cottage one more time, there will be something we both haven't thought of before."

Shona nodded, picking at the fabric of the plaid blanket. "I'm afraid for him. But ye believe me don't ye?"

"Aye. I believe he's not as much of a villain as MacLeod

deems, but I do also believe there is something in his past for which he's ashamed."

Shona swallowed around the lump that had formed in her throat. "I suppose we all have our secrets."

"Let us hope that we uncover his before MacLeod does."

They finished their meal, and then lay beneath the blanket of stars and the moon. Thoughts of Rory were pushed to the back of their minds when the headiness of the wine and the magic of the glen took hold once more. They made slow, leisurely love until they were both too drained to move or speak. They fell asleep beneath the sparking magic of the glen stone.

## 4

RORY

*Present Day*

Everything was loud. Very loud.

Rory MacLeod resisted the urge to cover his ears as he slowly stood and turned in a circle.

The smells... They were from another world. Smoke, but not like that of the peat fires he was used to. Cooking, but oddly oily. And ale. He smelled that, too.

Searing pain seeped through Rory's head, from one end to the next. He reached up to touch his temples, rubbing at the sensitive flesh covering his skull.

What in bloody hell happened?

He blinked opened his eyes to see that the world was dark, but not.

The sky above his head was black, dotted with a few sparkling stars and the occasional wisp of a cloud. But it should be completely dark, and yet the world seemed lit up by lights.

*Shite.*

He was back.

Suddenly on alert to what he thought might have happened, the pain in Rory's head grew, but he shoved it aside. Leaping to his feet, his leather boots thunked on the stone walkway. He reached for his sword at his hip, but it was gone, and he sort of remembered having yanked it from the scabbard when he'd first started to travel, believing he was under attack.

With a glance up and down the street, he took in the looming city buildings, and the lights that shone artificially inside and out. People were laughing and chatting. Carriages —nay automobiles?—whizzed past. There was an occasionally shouted, "Wanker!"

Turning slowly, he made out Edinburgh Castle, lit up in blue on the north side of the Royal Mile.

Dressed in his traditional Highland garb, he wouldn't be out of place with the other men who paraded themselves for these oddly modern people wearing the strangest clothes he still couldn't fully fathom—and this his second journey here. Their limbs were covered in fabric. It was neither hot nor cold.

*Journey.*

Lord, but that word made it sound so normal. So usual for a man from the year 1541 to pass through time and land here, on the cold stone, five hundred some odd years in the future.

The last time he'd journeyed, or rather time traveled, when he'd returned to his own time, the very next day, Shona arrived from the future. Lost, confused. As of now, she'd not yet regained her memory. But he'd known her before she arrived in 1538. Her sister, Moira, had been the one to take him in, right here in Edinburgh the last time—which had been for a year at least. He'd fallen in love with Moira, had wanted to stay with her forever. So many years he'd been searching for a way back to her and now he was finally here.

So, he'd taken care of Shona, because he cared for her like a sister and because that was what Moira would have wanted.

And then it hit him. *He was back*. Back to see her. Back to tell her how sorry he was for simply disappearing. To beg for her forgiveness. His excitement abated somewhat when he realized the repercussions of his journeying back and forth.

First of all, he'd left so unexpectedly, there'd been no time to tell her goodbye. She didn't even know he was a time-traveler. A secret he'd kept the entire year he'd been with her. She likely detested him for vanishing.

Unless he could be lucky enough to have magically appeared back in Edinburg just a few hours after disappearing.

He didn't have that kind of luck.

Luck be damned, he had to see her. Moira and Shona were close. However long it had been, she was most assuredly missing her sister. He needed to put her mind at ease, no matter how angry she might be. He had to put his own mind at ease. For the last three years he'd wandered the forests of Scotland wishing he could be back with her, the love of his life. His thoughts ate at him. Would she hate him? Would she love him still? Would she have fallen for another?

*Damn*. This meant Shona was on her own. No one to protect her. Did this signify that another was coming through in his time?

But who?

Moira? Could it be?

Rory could only hope. He'd been miserable without her.

"Bloody hell," he grumbled, turning in a circle to regain his bearings. It had been awhile since he'd been here and he wasn't sure he remembered where the hell he was exactly.

Down the Royal mile, to the right, around the bend, another right—or was it a left? At any rate, he would be walking for a good thirty minutes before he arrived at his destination.

"Nice kilt," a gaggle of females said, wiggling brows and leering lips. They were half-sotted.

"Dare ye to ask what's underneath," he challenged.

"Oh!" they drawled out, mouths popping open with excitement.

They reminded him of the tavern wenches back in Grant country—hungry for cock and coin.

"You are a naughty Highlander," one of the girls said sauntering forward. She licked her lips, pulling a multi-colored piece of paper from her pocket—their odd currency.

Well now, this was a change of pace... He could get paid to flirt? Why the hell not?

"Do ye know why the Scots wear kilts, lassie?" Rory teased.

She grinned, her fingers sliding over his belt. "Why?"

"Because the sheep can hear a zipper from a mile away." He'd heard that one on his last journey here. He'd not known what a zipper was but as soon as he found out, he'd laughed his arse off.

It took the lass a moment to process his crude joke, but as soon as she did, she and her friends burst out laughing. She tucked the bill into his belt, and said their goodbyes, giggling all the way down the street.

Rory tugged out the bill. £20.

*Nice.*

The last time he'd been here, he'd been lucky to get a job as a bartender at one of the local pubs. Well, if he was to stay long, and another bartender position didn't open up, he knew a good way to make some money. All he had to do was stand on the street corner telling dirty jokes to drunken lassies.

As appealing as that sounded, he had something he needed to do. Rory shoved the money into his sporran and took off at a brisk pace southward on the Royal Mile.

A number of years had passed since he'd been here before, but re-walking the path of the past seemed to come to him instinctively. Much like back in his own time where he could tell the difference in the many wooded, and moors, back-dropped routes. At least here, their pathways were labeled. Castle Wynd to Johnston. Johnston to Castle Terrace, then Spittal. Spittal to Bread and Morrison. Haymarket to Coates Gardens.

How the hell did they come up with those names anyway?

The walk was pleasant. Nearly half an hour, if he remembered correctly. He passed by alehouses, spritely groups of people. A few others dressed like him soliciting coin for entertainment. A few in a different, more modern looking Highland garb, jovial and proper as they journeyed onward. It was good to see that some men still dressed in their tartans rather than the odd blue woven fabric that Moira had called jeans.

Then he was there, standing in the middle of the street, looking up at the brick town house with a tin roof and pretty flowers that hung outside the windows in wood and iron boxes. Rory sighed deeply, crossed the street and was prepared to walk up the seven or eight steps when the door burst open, and a ball of fury flew out on the short patio, dark hair, a mass of riotous curls around her beautiful face. Blazing blue eyes, a regal nose and cherry-red lips that were meant to be kissed. Tall and fit, her body begged to be explored, and yet the way she was coming at him, he should have been scared for his life.

So much spirit. Just like her sister. She and Shona looked so much alike, too. Twins, though not exactly identical given their hair. If not for the color of their hair being different, anyone would have a hard time telling them apart. But he could. Rory could have told them apart blind folded. For their scents were different.

Shona smelled faintly of flowers, where Moira was altogether a spicier, citrus and vanilla scent. Lord, but he wanted to wrap her around him.

"Ye!" Moira seethed.

Rory let out another deep sigh, shaking himself from his thoughts. "I see ye remember me."

A low growl came from her pretty throat. He supposed a joke wasn't the right way to start of their reunion.

"Remember ye? Ye broke my heart and stole my sister." Hands skated over her face, shoving her hair from her flushed cheeks and she glanced up and down the street with her striking eyes.

She was just as gorgeous and fiery as he remembered. And hated him now. That was different and left what felt like a punch to the gut in his middle.

"Where is she?" Moira demanded.

"Shona?" What the hell was wrong with him? He couldn't seem to get his thoughts right. He just wanted to reach for her. Hold her.

"Who else would I be asking about? Unless ye've only come back to Edinburgh to seduce another lass."

"No. Not another." He'd only ever tried to seduce Moira. It had worked. He could still remember every night, her lush curves beneath him, over him, in front of him. The way her soft skin had felt under his fingertips, the heat of her mouth and the velvet of her tongue sliding over his turgid flesh. Rory shivered.

No use reminiscing, the lass hated his guts.

Her narrowed gaze focused on him, and instead of stepping back into her house to slam the door in his face, as he would expect any self-respecting lass to do, she stormed down the stairs coming within a few inches of him, her citrus and vanilla scent wrapping around him and once more setting his lustful memories to bloom.

"What the hell do ye want?" Then her eyes pricked with tears. "Where is she?"

Rory felt immediately guilty. Moira wouldn't understand his situation, that her sister was no longer in this time. How could he tell her without having her start screaming like a raving lunatic and calling the authorities to hall him off to the nearest dungeon?

"She is well and safe," he found himself saying.

"Where? Why hasn't she called? Or even gone medieval and written me a letter?"

Medieval. Good one. He didn't lie—exactly. "She's in Grant country. The phone service is bad there, and well... She has a tiny case of—" He searched for the word. He couldn't recall it; maybe he had a touch of it, too. All this time hopping couldn't be good on the brain. "Her memory is—"

"Ohmygod, you wiped her memory?" Now Moira raised her hands and backed up the stairs. "Get away from me, ye sicko. I'm calling the police, ye'll not get away with this."

"Wait, Moira." Rory followed her up the stairs, hands outstretched. "It's not that. I've not hurt her, I've been protecting her." He ran his hand through his hair with frustration and cursed under his breath. "I came here—" Why the hell had he come here? He should have known she wouldn't understand. He should have thought a moment, come up with a plan. How could explain it? It wasn't like he'd gotten a warning other than feeling dizzy and weightless. There wasn't some magical voice that said: *I'm sending you here for this reason.* Nay, he was simply sent, and the first thing he thought of when he got here was Moira. "I came here to get ye."

"To get me?" She laughed, but it was not a humorous

laugh. Nay, it was filled with derision. "Well, I'm not going to let ye *get me*. The only thing ye're getting is jail time."

"Moira, listen please." How the hell was he going to convince her? *Ballocks!* This had seemed so much easier when he'd been walking over here initially. "I'm not a criminal. I swear it."

She stared into his eyes, searching, and he could see pain there, he could see hope. But she shook her head at him, shuttering her emotions from his view. "I can't believe a word ye say, Rory. I trusted ye before. Trusted ye with my body, with my home, my sister. And the two of ye ran away together. Is that it? She can't be bothered to call me because she ran off with the guy I loved?"

"Ye loved me." It wasn't a question, but a statement.

Moira let out an annoyed groan. "Past tense, arsehole. I've moved on."

That stung. He didn't want her to have moved on to another man. Jealousy reared inside him, and if her new lover had been there, Rory would have pummeled him to the ground.

"Go back to Shona. I don't even know why ye came here."

Rory hung his head. Maybe this was a bad idea. He wasn't into self-torture. Maybe for her sake, he should just let her go. But he couldn't. His heart still beat for Moira and his blood still ran hot when he thought of her. He'd never fallen for Shona as Moira accused, only tried to protect her and help her get used to her new world five hundred years in the past. He couldn't control the Fates, or the Devil, whoever it was that ruled his journey as though he were a puppet. And somehow, he had to convince Moira of the truth, or else he wasn't going to be able to make it back to his time. At least, that seemed a likely result.

The sound of the door shutting had him looking up sharply. She'd gone inside. Not even said goodbye. He heard the click of her lock. She was shutting him out. And Shona, too. Did she truly believe her sister capable of such a thing? He could understand, even though it hurt, that she might think he would. After all, they might have known each other intimately—again and again—but they'd only been acquainted for a year or so before the time gods had yanked him back to the 1500's.

Judging by the placement of the moon, it would be midnight in a couple of hours. He didn't have any place to go tonight, but he could use a drink. A stiff whisky. If he recalled correctly, there was a tavern around the corner. He didn't want to go back to the place he'd worked, as they likely wouldn't serve him since he'd up and disappeared. He trudged back up the street until he found MacTavish's Tavern. Rory pushed open the door, studied the room to be certain he'd not find any trouble. There were only a few patrons so far, and none of them paid him any attention.

He approached the bar, pulled out a stool and sat.

"What can I get ye?" the barkeep asked.

"Whisky, make it a triple." Didn't matter what time period he was in, he could always order his whisky the same way.

The barkeep nodded, plunked down a medium sized glass cup and filled it to the brim with amber liquid.

"Ye look familiar," the barkeep said.

Rory nodded, and gulped down the entire contents of the cup in one swill. He tapped the cup on the bar and was rewarded with another pour. "I was here a year or so ago."

"Aye, I remember."

Rory drank down the second cup, feeling the whisky warm his belly.

"Ye were with the Ayreshire lassies, and ye worked at Dougal's."

Shona and Moira Ayreshire. They were popular in the area

for their herbal shop and their generosity. Everyone remembered them.

"Aye. Just came from Moira's house now."

"She was mighty displeased with ye, I reckon."

Did the whole town know his business? He supposed they would, at least those who worked and lived close to Moira.

"She was, but I'm hoping to reconcile." Rory grinned, though there was no happiness in it. He swallowed a large gulp of whisky loving the intense burn as it made its way down his throat.

"Might be damned near impossible. Where's her sister?"

He was expecting that.

"She's north, in Grant country, near Castle Gealach."

"Working?"

"Aye, at the castle actually." That was not technically a lie. She was working around there... five hundred years in the past.

"Castle Gealach? Ye don't say." The barkeep once more refilled Rory's cup.

"She's a natural. The people love her."

"And ye? Do ye love Shona?"

Rory looked the man in the eye. "She's like a sister to me. I'd protect her with my life."

"And Moira?"

The whisky was warming its way through his blood. He'd forgotten how much time-travel took out of him. Another swill and he might be well and truly drunk.

"I'm hoping..." He trailed off, not wanting to give away too much information about himself, his intentions.

"Ye like her."

"A lot." He admitted.

"Even love her."

Rory nodded.

"Well, good luck to ye. She's got another man now. A big one. And he's not likely to let her go so easily."

Rory grunted, a small bitter laugh escaping. "The good lassies are always scooped up, are they not?"

"Aye. But truth be told, ye can win her back. Dickie's a bit of an overbearing arsehole. His father is part owner of Scottish Airways, and he's let the power of all that cash get to his head."

Rory ran his hand through his hair. "And all I've got is a measly £20."

The barkeep chuckled. "Whisky's on the house. I always did like ye. And if ye promise to get that prick out of this side of town, I'll give ye free whisky for the rest of your days."

"What sort of trouble is he giving ye?" There had to be more to it than breaking the bastard up with Moira.

"Giving my lad some trouble, that's all. Him and his blokes. They don't live around here. Only come by to see Moira. My lad's the bar-back, and they rough him up a little every time they come by."

"It'd be my pleasure." Rory got up from his stool, wavering slightly on his feet. He needed to sleep.

"Thanks, mate." Then he called out, stopping Rory. "If ye need a job, I could use a bartender a couple nights a week to help me out."

Rory nodded. If he were here longer than a few days, then he'd need some cash. "Thanks for the offer. I'll let ye know." He trudged to the door, surprised his legs felt a bit wobbly. Whisky was doing its job making him feel numb.

A blessing it was MacTavish's was so close to the Ayreshire house, because he planned to sleep in Moira's back yard.

He prayed she'd already gone to bed. She'd most likely not be pleased with him creeping around again.

Rory smiled and stumbled his way down the street toward her house, half-hoping he'd run into the arsehole she was bedding down with.

## 5

MOIRA

Sleep had not come easy to Moira Ayreshire. She'd spent most of the night tossing and turning, wishing that she'd yanked open the door, after yelling at Rory and locking him out. She should have asked him to come inside. To tell her about her sister. To take her to Shona. To ask why he'd up and left; why he'd run away with her sister after a year of telling Moira he loved her.

Dressed in his kilt and boots, his white shirt clinging to the muscles of his chest and arms, the man made an impressive picture. The sight of him, unchanged since she'd last seem him, brought her tunneling back to when they'd been together. Every happy memory, and every heartbreak.

She flopped her arm over her face. He'd said something about Shona's memory. What was wrong with her sister? Amnesia?

Moira yanked back the blankets and trudged to the bathroom. She'd been so heartless to not even listen to him, to find out what happened. She just didn't know what to believe. How to feel. What to say.

The morning sun was starting to beam through the

window that looked out onto her small back lawn, her abundant garden lay dormant and her mini-green house was covered in dew.

She dazedly gazed down at her patio, a place she and Shona had sat in the evenings to drink wine and chat about their days. The very same patio she'd made love to Rory on when the sun had set and no one was the wiser.

Yanking on the curtains, she wanted to shut out the sight. But then her eye caught on something and she did a double take. Or rather *someone*.

"Ye've got to be kidding me," she grumbled.

Filling up the expanse of the chaise lounge furthest to the right was the six-feet-six figure of Rory. Dead asleep, one muscular arm thrown over his eyes. A long leg extended over the end of the chaise, and the other was hanging off the side. His long dark hair had come loose of his tie, streaks of the morning sun shining red through the charred wood color of it. His skin was still tanned, his chin strong, kissable lips surrounded by the dark hair of his goatee. Closed lids hid the most amazing eyes, the color of dark chocolate and espresso. Two of her favorite things.

Why did he have to look so damned sexy? Even in sleep she appreciated the shear beauty of him.

Though she was irritated, she also recognized the blessing in disguise at seeing Rory sleeping on her chaise. She raced to use the bathroom, brushed her teeth as though a motor were on her arm and then yanked on her robe. She didn't bother with slippers as she sped down the stairs, through her living room and kitchen to the back door. Flinging it open, she faced a startled Rory, who'd sat straight up and stared at her as though she were a total stranger and he had no idea where he was.

"Let me guess, ye've lost your memory, too? Let me

remind ye, this is my house, and ye're trespassing." She fisted her hands at her sides.

Ugh, why did she have to be so mean? She actually wanted him to stay so she could find out what happened to Shona! See how he was, though she shouldn't care.

Rory scrubbed a hand over his face, the dazed look vanishing and the determined set of his jaw showing.

"Is Dickie inside? Dinna want him to see an ex-lover of yours out here, do ye?" His tone was brutal and cut straight to her core.

"How do ye know about Dickie?" She'd not mentioned her boyfriend's name last night.

"Everyone knows about Dickie." Rory rolled his eyes.

"Everyone, who?" she challenged, hands on her hips, her robe parting enough that Rory stared at the way her nipples had hardened in the brisk morning air. She yanked her robe closed again.

Rory hid his grin but she saw it, and it made her all the more strident. She had to stick to her guns! No melting!

He stood, stretching, his long, muscled arms, reaching toward the dawn sky, his shirt, already loosened from his belt rising to show a glimpse of his chiseled abs.

Dear heavens, but he was still the most striking man she'd ever come across, and the best lover she'd ever had. The man had rocked her world and then left her alone in the aftermath. Involuntarily, she shivered as she remembered the expert way his hands had roved over her body, plucking, stroking, and tickling. This was *not* sticking to her guns...

"Eyes up here, love," Rory said.

*Dammit!* Moira had been staring at his cock. She yanked her gaze upward, glaring, only to find a satisfied grin on his face. Heat suffused her face and that only made her madder.

He winged a brow, his lip curling in a way that made her

want to slap him. "Your male friend is not satisfying ye in the bed chamber?"

"My love life is none of your concern," she seethed.

"Ye love him?"

She groaned, remembering the one annoying trait of his that he took everything so literally. "That is also none of your business."

Rory stepped forward, one muscular leg in front of the other, the rising sun hidden behind his incredible height and the air between them being sucked away before she could breathe.

"What if I make it my business?" His voice had grown deeper, more gravelly, the way it had right before he used to drag her toward his hard body and kiss her until she couldn't stand up straight.

Moira stepped away, trying to catch her breath. She had to think, had to remember why she'd stalked out here in the first place instead of calling the cops, but there he was, the heat of his body flush to hers, his fingers sliding behind her neck, and his mouth descending. She could do barely more than tilt her head back, part her lips, watch as he closed the distance between them and finally he was kissing her. Every inch of her screamed in revelry, in merriment for what she'd dreamt about the past three years.

The scent of him, spicy and male; the taste of him earthy and sensual. His tongue slicked over hers. She couldn't help but touch him, press her hands to his chest, breathe him in deep. He groaned, deepening the kiss, and Moira answered with a sound at the back of her throat that was a half-moan, half-whimper.

He pressed her back against the door, his body enveloping her in warmth and seduction. His arousal, thick and hard, pressed to the crux of her thighs.

And that was when she remembered she wanted to get

away from him, that he'd up and disappeared after making her believe he'd loved her for over three hundred and sixty-five days. Moira pressed her hands to his chest and pushed.

"Stop," she gasped.

Rory dragged his mouth from hers, but didn't let go; he touched his forehead to hers. "Anything for ye, love." His voice was husky, his dark eyes hooded, desire seeping through his stunning dark gaze.

"Stop calling me love. I'm not yours." And she wriggled another inch of space between the two of them.

"I've missed ye."

She wasn't going to let him seduce her into forgetting what she wanted, needed. "I want ye to bring Shona to me," she said. "I know ye said ye came to get me, but I can't leave with ye."

"Why?"

She glanced away, focusing on one of her flowerpots; it looked sad and empty since she'd yet to fill it.

"It's complicated," she answered.

"Dickie?"

Why did he have to bring Dickie into this? Dickie was nothing to her. A fling. Somebody to go out to dinner with, to have drinks with, or to sleep beside so she didn't feel so alone in the world.

"Let's not talk about Dickie."

"Why not?"

"Because, it's none of your business. Tell me about Shona."

"How about a cup of that black stuff. I canna remember what it was called. Not tea."

Moira rolled her eyes. "Coffee? I'm not an idiot. I know they have coffee in Grant country. I've been to Castle Gealach and drank it in the visitor's center."

Rory chuckled. "Ye haven't changed a bit."

Moira frowned, uncertain whether to be annoyed, offended or flattered, maybe all three. The way he said it sounded like a compliment, like he enjoyed her irritation, but a comment like that usually meant some sort of offense. So, which was it? Damn the man for being so confusing.

She crossed her arms protectively in front of her, tugging her robe tighter, feeling the need to pretend it was the cold that made her do it.

Rory stepped closer, and she felt herself moving backward until her back hit the door to her kitchen again.

"Let's not argue, *love*. I've not seen ye for a good long while. How about that coffee?"

Needing to put space between them before she reached up and threaded her fingers through his lush hair to see if it was just as silky as she remembered, Moira reached behind her, fumbling for the door handle.

"One cup, and ye'd better be explaining to me all that's happened in the past three years. I filed a missing person's report for my sister for crying out loud. And the cops, they're probably looking for ye, too."

He didn't respond, just stared at her. "Ye have no idea how much I've missed ye, Moira."

She could have melted. Could have slid right up against him the sound of his voice was so inviting. So instead, she whipped around and nearly fell onto her tiled kitchen floor in her haste to get away from him, and retorted, "Ye said that already."

"Looks the same," Rory said, nonchalantly stepping inside.

He walked to her cupboard and pulled out two cups. He'd not been bothered to remember her at all the last few years, so she tried not to care that he recalled the placement of her cups.

"Sit down. Don't touch anything."

Rory held his hands back, in an *I surrender* pose, and sauntered to her small, round kitchen table, unfolding his body into one of the chairs, dwarfing the piece of furniture.

Moira turned her back on him, working on the coffee, even though she felt wired enough from his presence to skip the caffeine altogether.

"Tell me about Shona," she encouraged as she dumped two lumps of sugar into each cup.

"Shona is well."

"Ye mentioned that yesterday," she said, trying to keep the irritation from her voice. "But I want to know more. Why didn't she contact me? It's been years, I thought she was dead." *Ohmygod, what am I doing? She could be dead and her murderer sitting right here in my kitchen!*

Moira jerked her gaze toward Rory, taking him all in. She'd never been afraid of him before, and even given the circumstances, she was surprisingly not afraid of him now.

"Ye have nothing to fear of me, lass," he whispered. "I know none of this makes sense, and it barely makes sense to me either, but ye have to listen. Ye have to trust me."

Moira carried the steaming cups to the table and handed him his. Their fingers brushed for the faintest of moments, but it still sent spirals of pleasure and excitement racing over her wayward limbs. She shook her head, disappointed that three years, a whole lot of torment and her missing sister hadn't made her more cautious—or at the very least, taken away her desire for the man.

"I will listen," was the only answer she was willing to give.

Rory cleared his throat, and then took a giant gulp of his coffee, wincing as the heat burned his tongue. Her first reaction was to reach forward and touch his hand in comfort, but before her fingertips made contact, she yanked them back. He'd seen her movement and gazed at her with longing in his eyes.

Moira swept her hair back and pretended it hadn't happened.

One slight raise of his brows told her he wasn't going to pretend.

"Well?" she said, trying to push past her instincts to touch him.

Rory sighed. "Three years ago, something happened. Before I met ye, I—" Abruptly he stopped and leapt to his feet. "Someone's here."

How could he know, no one had even knocked—and then the front door shuddered beneath a heavy-handed bang. Suddenly, her belly was flipping up toward her throat. "Dickie." She forgot all about telling him she'd go for a jog with him before breakfast. The tea-tasting room and spice shop she and her sister owned—well, mostly her now that Shona had disappeared—was closed today. Her only day off during the week.

Rory started to walk toward the front door, but Moira scrambled from her chair, grabbing hold of his arm. He glanced down at her with thunder in his expression. Dear Lord, how did she stop an angry, jealous, possibly murderous Highlander from attacking her current boyfriend?

"Stop," she hissed. "Just don't. Dickie..." She trailed off, not knowing how to say that the man she dated was a jealous arse when it came to competition. Hmm... Much like Rory.

"I've heard about Dickie." Pure disdain filled his voice.

"So ye said," she murmured. "Let me answer the door. Ye hide."

"Hide?" His expression turned incredulous. "I dinna hide from anyone."

Moira tightened her hold on his arm, positioning herself between him and the front door. "Please, for my sake?"

"What? Why would this man be angry?"

Thinking quickly, she raised her brows, and said, "What

would ye think if ye came to fetch a lass ye'd laid claim to and found her in her robe, in the wee hours of the morn, drinking coffee with another bloke?"

His expression dawned understanding. "Ah, I see. Where should I hide?"

The door shuddered again beneath Dickie's fist. "Moira! Open up! I can hear ye talking in there."

"Oh, jeez," she said, hating the panic that raced through her blood. She'd done nothing wrong. Rory was a guest, nothing more.

Even if she did feel the heat of his muscled arm beneath her fingertips and even if that feeling led to rather sordid memories of them falling into bed, or up against a wall.

"The cellar. Hide in the cellar." She tugged him toward the small door that led down to the old, dank cellar. A place she never went because it was too damned scary.

She yanked open the door, and tried to stuff his bulk through the small entry. "Go!"

Rory chuckled. "I'll not make a peep."

Moira rolled her eyes. "Ye'd better not, else Dickie decides he wants to take up mixed martial arts instead of running."

She quietly shut the cellar door in the face of his confusion. Did he truly not know what MMA was?

Rushing to the door, she opened it up just as Dickie was about to bang again.

"Babe, what took ye so long?" he asked.

She smiled, hoping her face didn't show her worry. "Sorry, was on the phone."

"Who with? It's so early."

Without thinking, she said, "Shona. Turns out she's been up north the past few years. Fell ill with amnesia and couldn't tell anyone who she was."

"Wow. That's a relief." He tugged her forward and planted

a kiss on her mouth—which felt extremely lacking compared to the one she'd just shared with Rory. He maneuvered himself inside. "Why aren't ye dressed?"

"I've been on the phone forever. I'm so sorry, I'm going to have to cancel our run."

"What?" His eyes flashed anger. "Ye haven't seen or heard from her in three years and now ye're going to give up on our plans because she called?"

Moira ignored the selfish tone, and calmly explained, even though it was a lie. "I'm going to see her. I'm sorry. It's not that I'm giving up on our plans, but my sister, she's been sick. She needs me."

Why was she still dating Dickie? He was such an arsehole.

"Moira—"

She cut him off with a gentle stroke on his arm. "Please, don't take this personally, Dickie. I promise I'll call while I'm away, and as soon as I'm back, we'll get together."

He shook his head, looking obstinate. Moira reined in her temper when she was ready to smack him.

"I'll come with ye."

"No!" she said a bit too loudly.

Dickie's face screwed up the way she'd seen it do when he didn't get what he wanted, though not normally directed at her. She wasn't sure why with him she couldn't speak her mind. She'd never had that problem with Rory, and in fact, Rory seemed to enjoy her bossing him around a bit. Not so, with Dickie, if he was denied anything, he became irate. The problem with a privileged life she supposed.

"What?" he asked faintly.

Moira swallowed, and tried to offer him an easy smile that felt forced. "I haven't seen her in so long, so I would really like to go by myself at first. Ye understand, don't ye?"

"I don't like it," he grumbled. "But I suppose it's fine."

Changing the subject he said, "Is that coffee? Can I have a cup?"

Ugh, she was hoping he would just leave, but having already disappointed him once, she decided what could it hurt? Rory would simply have to stay put a few minutes longer.

"Yes, of course, come on."

Dickie walked behind her, rubbing her shoulders as they went into the kitchen.

"I'll get ye a cup." She reached up for the cabinet.

"What the hell is this?" Dickie held up Rory's cup.

*Dammit!* She'd forgotten all about it.

"Why do ye have two cups of warm coffee sitting here?"

Moira swallowed, then let out a nervous laugh. "Oh, that's nothing." She grabbed him a cup. "I was so shocked on the phone with Shona that I forgot I'd already poured myself a cup and ended up pouring two." She moved to the coffee maker, pouring the liquid into his cup. "Honestly, I can be so dumb sometimes. One lump or two?"

Dickie came up behind her, grabbing her hips and grinding his crotch against her arse. "How about these two lumps?" He squeezed her butt.

No way was she going to have sex with him with Rory in the house. No freaking way! Besides, Rory had hit the nail right on the head when he suggested that she wasn't being satisfied in bed. Dickie had a great body, but that was about it. Not a bit of skill, and his selfishness tended to trump her pleasure. Again, why was she still with him?

Turning in his arms, she playfully swatted at him. "Stop it. Here ye go."

Dickie eyed her as though he were trying to figure out what she was hiding, and then took the cup, sauntering to the table and sitting in the same chair that Rory had.

"So, if she's gotten her memory back, why didn't she just come home?" He frowned, looking into his cup. "No cream?"

"Oh, sorry, forgot." She grabbed the jug from the fridge and brought it to the table, not bothering to offer him one of the fresh scones she'd baked the day before. She didn't want him staying more than this cup. "Looks like she just"—she raised her hands up in the air in question—"woke up, or whatever they call it."

"Hmm. Interesting." Dickie took a sip of the coffee and then stared into the cup in disappointment. He set it on the table.

"Scary is more like it." Moira shoved her fingers through her hair. "I hope it's not genetic or something."

"Most people get amnesia from an accident. Did she say if she was in an accident?"

The cellar door pushed open, silently, an inch behind Dickie's head, and Moira nearly choked on her own tongue.

## ❧ 6 ❧

### RORY

**B**allocks, but Rory wanted to open up the cellar door all the way. He'd cracked it enough to get a look at the jackanapes giving Moira a hard time. The moment the bastard had knocked—nay, banged—on the front door, Rory had despised him.

What a load of shite!

The arrogant man had walked into her domain as though he owned the place. Made demands. Interrogated her. If Rory hadn't known the two of them were involved, he would have thought one of the king's agents had knocked down her door in search of answers to some crime.

It took every ounce of his patience not to push the door the rest of the way open, grab the fool by his neck and pull him from the blasted chair. *His* chair.

*His* woman.

The sense of possession filled him so greatly, he had a hard time breathing. Moira was *his*. Even if she was denying him at the moment. She'd been his since the moment he laid eyes on her three years before. He'd spent the last three years in his own time trying to figure out just how to get back to her—on the pretense that he wanted to bring Shona back to where she belonged, but who was he kidding. He'd really wanted Moira. To see her, touch her, hear her laugh, to make love to her all night long and wake up beside her peaceful body in the morning.

"Yes, an accident," Moira was saying, her frown deepening as she concentrated on *Dickie*.

Fucking Dickie had better get his arse up and out of the house if he knew what was good for him.

There had been a split second where she'd spied Rory and he thought she was going to leap from her skin and blow his hiding spot, but she'd easily returned her focus to the arsehole sipping coffee as though it were wine, swishing it around his damned mouth like a ninny.

Saints, but Rory wished that in addition to time traveling he had the ability to read minds, or at the very least whisper into her head. He wanted to give her the strength to boot this bloke out. The strength to kick him in the ballocks, too.

The interrogation continued, and Rory was about to pitch the door open when her telephone actually did ring.

"Oh," Moira breathed out, leaping from her chair.

Dickie stood, too, and for a moment, Rory had the sense the man was going to answer the phone for her, but he could see the hesitation in Dickie's movements. At least the spoiled rat wasn't a complete fool.

"Hello?" A moment passed, and all the color drained from Moira's face. "Shona?"

The phone started to slip, her legs to buckle.

Rory was bursting through the cellar door and catching Moira just as her body fell to the floor, completely ignoring the rage-filled shout from Dickie.

"Moira?" Rory stared into her face, eyes closed, skin pale. He grabbed up the phone. "Hello?"

Dickie was quick to grab it before Rory could hear who

was on the other end, and he wasn't about to drop Moira in the process of fighting him for it. The bastard threw the phone toward the front of the house and bellowed at Rory, "Who the hell are ye?"

Rory sent the man a scathing look. He didn't need to explain a damned thing. He lifted Moira up and carried her into the living room, settling her on the couch, then turned to face off with the bastard.

"I asked ye a direct question," Dickie shouted.

"And I deliberately ignored ye." Rory smirked at the indignation his retort brought to the arsehole's face.

"Tell me who ye are and why ye're touching my woman."

"She was mine first." Rory grinned, satisfaction filling him to brimming when Dickie's face grew boiling red.

"Get the fuck out of here."

"Why dinna *ye* get the fuck out of here," Rory growled.

They both stood, fists clenched, chests heaving, teeth bared, about to pounce on the other when the phone rang once more.

Rory sprang toward the front of the house where Dickie had tossed the phone, but Dickie was right behind him. The two of them momentarily got stuck in the doorway in their haste to get to the phone first.

"Move!" Dickie shouted.

Rory didn't bother with shouting. He wrenched back his arm, and landed a crack on Dickie's temple with his elbow that had him crumpling to the floor of the kitchen in a deep sleep. "Ye move, bloody cur," Rory muttered.

He picked up the phone, forgetting only momentarily to hit the button that made the voices speak on the other end. "Hello?"

"R—Rory? Ohmygod, is that ye, Rory?"

Holy hell, was it really Shona? He'd have recognized her voice anywhere—but here?

"Aye, but... how? Shona?"

"I can't believe it!" There was a thudding sound and then a deep male voice said, "Who is this?"

"'Tis Rory, who is this?"

The man cleared his throat. "'Tis Ewan. Ye're a wanted man."

Wanted man? Rory shook off the accusation, his mind still reeling at hearing Shona's voice. How the hell had she time traveled and how did she know he'd be here? "Who are ye?"

"Shona's husband."

"Husband? When the bloody hell did that happen? Never mind. How are ye here, in this time?"

There was a deep sigh from the connection, a sound that Rory knew well.

"One minute we were asleep, and the next, we woke up on a strange road, surrounded by people with flashing lights."

"Flashing lights? What color?" Cameras, or police? Or flashlights?

"Blue and red. 'Twas the um... The guards. Their vehicle said police. Damn... I should have remembered all this." There was another frustrated sigh on the other end, and Rory had a feeling Ewan was struggling with what had happened. And who wouldn't? "They shackled us, threw is in a barred cell and they keep telling us we're indecent and that we only had one phone call to make. What the hell is a phone? Is this a phone? God, I should remember, but I canna. And why would we be indecent? Have they never seen a man's arse afore?"

"Take it easy, Ewan. I'll help ye. Where are ye?" Rory had been lucky enough not to end up in prison on his previous visit, though he'd gotten close a couple of times.

There was a muffled sound and then Shona was back on the line, her voice groggy. "We're at Saughton. Can ye tell

Moira to come pick us up? Tell her to hurry. There are a lot of creepy people in here and well, we're both sort of panicked at what's happened."

"Aye, of course. She had quite a shock. Passed out. I'll try to wake her."

"Thank ye, Rory. I'm glad to hear your voice. It's been so long."

"It's hardly been more than a day," Rory wiped a hand through his hair.

"Wow... Three years have passed."

"Three years?" Rory's head reeled. "I suppose that's how ye found a husband."

Shona laughed softly. "I wish they served whisky in this place."

"We'll bring some."

"And... we need some street clothes."

"All right."

Dickie started to rouse on the floor, moaning like a little bairn.

"I'll try to wake Moira." And get her bastard *ex*-lover out of there.

"Thank ye, Rory. I missed ye. I'm so glad ye're safe."

"I missed ye, too. I'm so sorry to have up and left ye so quickly. If I'd known..."

"Dinna blame yourself. We don't get a choice with Fate. Ye disappeared. But now we've found ye."

Disappeared. She didn't say left, or abandoned her, but disappeared. There was a whole subset of connotation with such carefully chosen words. "Ballocks..." he grumbled under his breath. "We'll be there soon."

"Thank ye so much."

Rory set the phone down, and then grabbed hold of Dickie's shirt at the nape of neck. "Time to take out the trash," he said in a singsong voice, then dragged the groaning man toward the door. He wasn't small, though nearly Rory's height, his muscular bulk was impressive. When he wasn't bossing women around, he must have concentrated on his build. "Nice to have made your acquaintance. Dinna come back. Ever." And with that, Rory tossed the man out the front door, bolted it, and returned to the living room where Moira was starting to rouse.

At first, she looked startled, eyes darting about before settling on him.

"Where is Dickie?"

"He had to make an untimely departure."

She frowned, and touched her forehead. "Ye threw him out didn't ye?"

"Aye." Rory grabbed her coffee mug from the kitchen table and brought it to her.

Moira took the cup and drank deeply before handing it back. "What happened? I dreamt that Shona..." She rubbed at her temples, closing her eyes in pain.

"She did. We have to go get them."

"Get who?"

"She brought a friend back with her."

"A friend."

"An Ewan."

Her eyes widened. "But I thought..."

"I told ye, Shona is not the Ayreshire lass for me, and she never was."

Her cheeks colored slightly, and she sat up, her gaze turned away from him.

Rory settled in front of her, his hands grasping hers at her knees. "Moira, there is so much I need to tell ye, but it will be best with Shona here, so ye dinna think..."

"That ye're lying?" she finished.

He nodded. "What I have to tell ye, our story, it is not believable to most people."

She waved away his words. "Let's go. I'll go change real quick." Moira let go of his hands and stood.

He nodded, rising to his feet. Patience was key. She wasn't ready to hear what he had to say, and that was all right. He could wait as long as she needed. "They require clothes."

"What?" She sounded so adorable when she was exasperated.

"Seems they traveled nude."

Moira rolled her eyes. "Not funny. I just fainted. Ye showed up on my door with some fantastical story about amnesia, then my sister called, then ye tossed my boyfriend out onto the street. I'm not in the mood for anything else."

"I jest not. And I think 'tis safe to say, Dickie is no longer your male friend."

"Ugh," she groaned, pushing to her feet. "Stop it."

"I'm entirely serious, lass. They are in jail for being indecent, of all things."

"Ohmygod. I can't deal with this! She probably didn't even call." Moira shoved past him. "That was not a nice trick, Rory. I know I haven't seen ye in a long time, but I expected better."

She didn't believe him, and he didn't blame her. Rory dropped to his knees, and held his hand over his heart. Moira turned around slowly to stare at him as though he'd grown not one but two extra heads.

"I swear to God, the almighty, and whatever else ye believe in, Shona needs us and she and her companion need clothes."

Moira pursed her lips. Hands on her hips. Several moments lapsed and he was certain she would demand he leave the same way Dickie had, when she finally spoke. "Fine. But if ye're messing with my head, I'm going to kick your arse back to Grant country."

Rory nodded. "A fine deal."

"Get changed. As much as I adore your kilt, ye'll stand out like a sore thumb at Saughton. I still have some of your old clothes."

"Ye kept them?"

"Don't get sentimental on me. My patience is worn so thin it's bleeding."

He chuckled. "Damn, I've missed ye, love."

"And stop calling me *love!*"

That only made him laugh harder, and she groaned loudly as she stomped all the way upstairs. He waited at the bottom of the staircase, not trying to push his luck, even though he wanted nothing more than to charge up the steps into her bedroom and toss her onto the bed to show her just how much he'd missed her.

A second later, fabric was flying toward him, as she tossed his clothes down the flight.

"Get changed!" she ordered.

"Aye, Madam General."

Her groan of irritation left him with a smile as wide as his face. Lord, he loved to tease the woman.

Rory made quick work of changing out of his clothes and then folded up his plaid and *leine* shirt together with his sporran. She'd not tossed down any undergarments, and the denim pants were snug against his half rigid cock. He was probably going to walk around with a hard-on for the rest of his time here.

"Ready?"

He turned around to see her standing there, a black bag in hand, thick, dark gray hose and a wool dress that came mid-thigh. Her feet were encased in leather boots much like his and her gaze was roving hungrily over him.

"Never more," he said, his voice husky. "And always." Without hesitating, he closed the distance between them, taking note of the hitch in her breath.

He couldn't help it. Knew she'd asked him to stop earlier, but the craving in her eyes, the pulsing heat between the two of them, he was helpless to it. And she didn't move. Didn't back away. In fact, he could have sworn she leaned forward, inching closer. Before she could push him away, he had to show her how much he missed her, and know how much she missed him in return, prove that she was lying to herself. Prove that he mattered more than the arsehole he'd tossed on his ear.

In one swoop, his mouth captured hers, one arm circled her back, hauling her up against him and the other hand threaded through her long, wild locks around the base of her skull. He claimed her mouth, demanding her attention, her response, opening her up to him and delving deep. His tongue slid over hers, tasting the mint of her tooth-wash, delighting in the tingle of it on his own tongue.

Her body was warm and supple pushed against him. Her breasts pert and full, the fabric of her gown not able to hide the hardness of her nipples. He fisted his hand at her back to keep from shredding her clothes from her body. His cock pushed painfully against his jeans, demanding to be let loose and his mind ran away with the memory of her slick channel, the tightness of her cunny and how he wanted so desperately to thrust deep inside her.

*Mo chreach.*

He slid his hand from the small of her back to the side of her hip, to her thigh as he walked her backward toward the wall. Her back pressed to the sturdy façade, he lifted her lithe thigh around his hip and ground his cock against the heat searing him between her delicious legs. Her body hadn't changed much in the past three years, maybe more fit. Her hips were still lush as lush as he recollected, her breasts... Oh, he had to touch her. He slipped his hand from her hair to cup a breast, feeling the hardened nipple against his palm. Sweet delight. He wanted her so badly. Might, in fact, take her right here against the wall.

He'd done so before. Many times.

He gently pinched her nipple as he ground against her, rocking his body back and forth, stirring his blood and hers. His denim was growing mighty damn uncomfortable. When she let out a soft whimper, he pinched a little harder, tilted his head and kissed her harder, sucking on her tongue the way he wanted to suck on that perky, pink nipple. He knew just what color it would be, like a dusky sunset set on cream.

Moira moaned, and he couldn't help but growl and press his cock harder against her sweet sex, the pleasure pulsing through him intense. He bit down on her lower lip, sucked, and then she did the same to him, mimicking every move he made.

"I want ye," he whispered against her mouth. "Ye were mine once, and ye'll be mine again." Rory dropped to his knees in front of her, slid his hands up under her dress, hooked his thumbs in the waistband of her hose, and tugged them down.

She didn't protest.

"Something to make ye remember me. Us," he growled. He drew the small triangle of her lacy underwear aside, revealing the sweet treasure he sought, and then he pressed his lips to her heat.

## 7

MOIRA

**P**otent desire filled Moira.

Pleasure, remembered and renewed, lit between her thighs as Rory lapped at her folds, worshipping her body. A body that pulsed only for him. No man had ever made love to her the way Rory did. No man compared. His enthusiasm, his talent—

*Oh!* His tongue swirled over her clit, then down, between her lips and back again.

Thank god for the wall behind her, because her legs shook hard enough she was certain she'd not be able to stand on her own.

Need and desire made her wet, made her skin tingle. She clenched her fists, trying to resist. They had things to do. She should push him away. Letting him touch her was wrong... But this... This seemed infinity more important at the moment. And it felt so damned right.

"Ye taste just as good as I remember," he murmured against her flesh, and the vibrations of it sent a new wave of pleasure coursing through her.

"Rory," she whimpered, fisting one hand in his hair. But

she was weak to her desire, her need, and the deep-seated emotions that he brought out. She wanted him. Missed him so much. And now he was here, and she was lost.

Sensing her surrender, he upped his pace, his tongue whipping pleasure against her clit. His calloused hands massaging and stroking her thighs.

She was a prisoner to her own cravings. Unable to move. Unable to breathe. Unable to think. Only seeking the end result of his delicious torment.

And then her body, alight with vigor and rekindled excitement, burst into fiery flames. Moira cried out, her hips bucking forward, limbs jerking, body shuddering. She grasped for something, anything to hold onto—his hair, the door behind her.

"Just like I remember," he said, sliding his mouth down the length of her inner thigh. "So intense, so honest. I love watching ye come."

She opened her eyes, looking down at him, and a flood of memories filled her. Maybe it was because of the vulnerable state she was in, or that he could so easily undo her, how with one look from him, she'd wanted to do whatever he said—and with a smile. Tears welled in her eyes.

Embarrassment at her tears, at how she'd let him go down on her, flooded through her senses and she moved to tug up her panties, her leggings and then shoved down her sweater dress. Rory sat back on his heels, looking confused.

"Go wash your face," she muttered, mostly disappointed in her own easy surrender. "We have to leave, if my sister really is in jail."

"Moira." He stood, and when she tried to turn around, he gently held onto her arms, sliding up to her shoulders so she was forced to face him. "What's wrong?"

She gritted her teeth, frustration filling her. "Ye. This. Us. *Everything!*" Hot anger burned her chest, and she couldn't hold it in anymore. "Ye've been gone for three years. *Three years*. Do ye realize that? In case ye didn't notice, that's a damned long time without any word. And to top it all, ye ran off with my sister. *My sister*. If ye knew what I'd been thinking, all the things I imagined..." Her voice broke off on a sob, and she quickly covered her face with her hands so he couldn't see her tears truly shed. "Ye can't just come back and expect me to fuck ye with a smile and a thank ye."

"Moira." Pain filled his expression and he looked torn. Genuine. As though his leaving hadn't been his fault. But how could she believe that? It was bullshit!

Rory gathered her in his arms, and once more, she allowed his touch, sinking into the vast expanse of his broad chest and the comfort of his thick muscles.

He was her weakness.

She laid her head against his chest, hearing the hitch in his heartbeat—not the only clue he was as affected as her. He held her tight, as though he didn't want to let go, and truly, she didn't want him to.

"If I could go back, if I could somehow be certain we wouldn't have left, I would have. Ye'll see when we talk to Shona, there was no choice. I didna want to leave ye, lass. I would have stayed with ye forever, and I canna tell ye how much I tried to get back to ye. How much I wanted to get word to ye. When I arrived yesterday—ye were the first thing on my mind. The only person I came to see, and even when ye pushed me away, I couldn't leave ye."

"I just don't understand." She lightly pounded at his chest as tears soaked his shirt. "Why?"

His chin moved back and forth on top of her head as he shook it. "I canna explain without Shona. Even Ewan will be able to help."

"Were ye kidnapped? Who held ye against your will?"

"Let us go, lov—lass, and soon ye'll know everything."

She'd be crazy to walk out the door with him. Crazy to let herself fall once more under his spell. Their relationship had been intense. And when he'd disappeared, it had broken her. She'd been dragging herself through life, settling for a relationship with Dickie because even though he was an arsehole, he was safe. He had his own money, he had his own life, and he didn't care enough to notice how broken she was.

"Please, Moira, let me have a chance to explain. Let me reunite ye with your sister." His dark eyes pleaded, and she caved.

Well, she supposed she was crazy. Obviously. Because, the thought of seeing her sister again, of hearing the truth from them all, was too much of a lure. She had to know. She'd never forgive herself if she didn't at least try. And, she'd be lying to herself if she didn't admit that the chance to be with Rory again didn't rank high on her list of motivations.

When they'd been together before, she'd been certain they were the real deal, the wedding bells, babies and a dog, kind of deal.

"Ye broke my heart," she said. "But I've no choice except to trust ye right now."

"I swear to ye, Moira, I'm going to make it up to ye. I'm going to heal your heart."

That made her frown and the stubborn side of herself, the piece that didn't want him to know how much he hurt her or how much she cared, glowered up at him. "What makes ye think I need *ye* to heal my heart?"

Rory held his hands up. "I'd never presume, lass. Never. I just want to show ye how sorry I am. I want to earn your forgiveness."

Moira let out a shuddering sigh. Her eyes were swollen, her face felt warm, no doubt she looked like a hot mess. But she had no other choice, and the hope that her sister was safe, charged her full of energy. She nodded, unable to say anything in regards to what he'd confessed. There was just too much, and she was afraid she'd start sobbing again. "I'll drive," she said softly.

Rory stared at her a moment, and then he, too, nodded. "Ye have the clothes?"

"Right here." She lifted the black duffle bag from the floor where she'd dropped it.

Rory unbolted the door and pulled it open for her. "After ye, my lady."

Moira hid her tiny smile. Even now, after all this time, he was still a gentleman.

As she stepped out onto the porch, she had a moment of panic where she expected to see Dickie storming toward them. But he was nowhere to be seen. Part of her felt bad for Dickie. He'd been literally tossed out of her house. He might have deserved it a little, but still... She also knew there would be some sort of backlash. Dickie was a lot of bluster, but when he sought his revenge he liked to fly under the radar. She'd probably find out all her sky miles were wiped clean or something, or something equally passive aggressive that she couldn't pin on him.

"I remember this carriage," Rory said, walking straight up to her compact, red car.

"Do ye remember how to use it?"

He laughed and shook his head. "I dinna think ye want me to try." He took the bag from her and tossed it into the backseat.

Moira couldn't help a quiet laugh, recalling what had happened the last time she'd let him drive. On a whim, they'd gone out to the country so she could teach him. They'd ended up driving through a fence onto a random farm with dogs chasing them, chomping at the wheels as they screamed for the dogs to leave them be until they made their way to a road again.

"Yeah, I'm good with driving," she said. "I think seeing my sister is going to be enough excitement for me." Immediately her mind was inside her foyer, thinking of the excitement they'd just had.

She shuddered, and moved jerkily to grab her door handle, but there Rory was, opening the car door for her, too.

"Allow me," he said, his voice whisper soft, and his breath warm near her ear.

"Thanks," she said, rather roughly, trying to get over the way he made her feel—which wasn't working in the least.

She settled into her seat, buckled up, and started the car, while Rory worked to fold himself inside. This all felt so unreal. Like she was floating in a dream, except, her head pounded with the beginning of migraine. It had to be reality. Rory finally got himself into the car, his knees pressed to the dash and his head touching the roof.

Moira pressed her lips together to keep from laughing. She'd forgotten what a challenge it was for a man with Rory's height to fit in her car. He looked like a giant, and at six-feet-six, he practically was.

Finally, he remembered how to push the seat back to a point where he had more room to sit.

"I hope Ewan isn't as tall as ye are," she said.

"I've never met the man."

"My sister brings a strange man home, and ye've been with her the past few years and ye don't know who he is?" She raised a doubtful brow at him, and then looked past his shoulder to see if there were any cars coming.

Coast was clear. She pulled out onto the street. The drive was quick, perhaps fifteen or twenty minutes after they got past being stuck at every light, and waiting for hordes of pedestrians to cross in front of them. Those minutes ticked by like an eternity of time. They were both quiet, contemplating. She wondered what it would be like to see her sister. Rory said, for some reason. Shona and her companion had been without clothes. How the hell had that happened?

Moira turned into the prison parking lot, the tall brick building looming up foreboding behind barbed wire, and she had a sudden fear of going inside. She didn't want to. This was a scary place, filled with criminals.

"Saughton Prison," she murmured. When they were kids, living in a foster home, anytime they were bad or tried to run away, their foster parents would warn that one day they'd be housed in Saughton Prison.

How right they were.

Holy hell.

"Let's get this over with." Moira shoved open her door and Rory grabbed the bag from the backseat. "Did she mention bail?"

Rory shook his head. "Not that I remember."

"I brought my checkbook in case."

Moira didn't remember her parents, and all she had left of them was a sizable trust fund that every foster home they'd gone through had been determined to mine as though it were gold. Luckily for her and Shona, the powers that be had seen that the money was safely held until the two of them came of age, and then only incrementally. They'd been sent to college, their bills paid by the lawyers in charge of the trust, and spending money put into their accounts. Their house had been paid for, and the money they received even now was only meant to supplement their own incomes, unless of course there was an emergency. Like now. This was definitely an emergency.

Her feet refused to move, pinned to the ground where she stood.

Rory came up beside her, the heat of his body comforting. He slid his fingers into hers. "I'll be right beside ye."

"I know." She glanced up at him and smiled wearily. "Thank ye."

He opened his mouth, no doubt to say something magnanimous and chivalrous, but Moira shook her head.

"Don't say anything. I need to process this. Let's walk."

They headed toward the entrance, the wall of windows reflecting the sun, making them appear to shimmer silver.

Once inside, they signed in, and luckily, in addition to his clothes, she'd kept Rory's wallet with his ID, which he'd left on the bedside stand the morning he'd disappeared.

As they sat to wait, Moira's hands trembled. Shona was here. The guard would have said no if she wasn't. Wouldn't she?

A few moments later, they were led to a small room, sans the bag, as they were not allowed to bring it in for security reasons—even though it had been searched.

*This is it. This is real.*

The door opened, and standing in the middle of the room, each wearing a pair of dark gray sweatpants and a light blue t-shirt, were Shona and her male companion. Shona looked just as Moira remembered. Wild, red hair in a mass of curls surrounding a face that was like looking in the mirror. Her companion rivaled Rory's height and was handsome in a fierce sort of way, though his smile was genuine. In coloring, where Rory was dark, Ewan was light.

Tears sprang to Moira's eyes and her hands were once more covering her mouth as though her body involuntarily wanted her to be quiet, to not say a word, to hold everything in.

Shona spoke first, shouting out, "Moira!" and rushing forward, her fiery-red hair bouncing, to grab her in a squeeze so tight she pressed the air from her lungs. "Ohmygod, I had no idea how much I missed ye until I remembered ye."

Moira held her sister tight, her mind spinning.

"I'm so glad ye're safe," Moira said over and over again. "I'm so glad."

Shona held her sister at arm's length, tears in her eyes, too, but a smile split her face from ear to ear. "I cannot believe all that has happened."

Beside them, Rory and Ewan shook hands, speaking in low tones.

"Tell me everything," Moira said. "Why did ye leave? Why didn't ye tell me? What happened?"

Shona shook her head. "There is so much, and I fear ye will not believe most of it. Let's get out of here and I'll tell ye everything."

Moira could barely walk. Her feet were tingling, her legs were shaking, and she was even a little dizzy. She swayed on her feet.

Rory rushed to her side. "One faint is enough for today," he teased, holding her up with a hand on her elbow.

"I'm Ewan," the man beside Shona said.

"Moira. I'm glad to meet ye." She held out her hand to shake his, but he shook her forearm instead. Odd.

The way Shona looked up at him made Moira's heart ache. They were in love.

"We brought ye clothes, but they wouldn't let us bring it in." Moira swept tendrils of her hair behind her ear with trembling fingers.

"'Tis all right, the clothes we've got on are not that bad, though the pants are a big snug." Ewan shifted uncomfortably.

"Just wait until ye try denim, my friend," Rory replied. "Not at all forgiving on the unmentionables."

That made Moira laugh, though it sounded sharp to her ears. Shona laughed softly, slipping her hand into her husband's grasp.

"Hate to break up your party, but we need the room for

the next visitor. Head to processing and they'll get ye checked out," a guard said from the doorway.

"Thank ye," Rory said to the guard, and started to usher them all out of the room.

Shona and Ewan did not have any personal articles, so there was nothing more to do but pay the bail fee. Moira's hand shook as she wrote the check, the numbers coming out fuzzy. The guard studied her, uneasily.

"Are ye all right, ma'am?"

"Nerves," Moira answered, the understatement of the year. In less than twenty-four hours, her entire world had changed. Again. She turned away from the guard and stared once more at her sister, who looked as healthy as could be, and happier than she'd ever seen her. Seemed unfair almost.

"There are bathrooms by the doors. Ye both could change if ye wanted to," Moira said again, still concentrating on the clothes, unable to focus on anything deeper.

Shona grabbed her hand. "Take us home, sis."

## ❦ 8 ❧

### MOIRA

They all managed to squeeze into the small car somehow, and Moira drove on automatic back to the house she'd shared with her sister. Inside the car was silent, but not uncomfortably so. It was as if everyone subconsciously knew that each of them needed some time, and theoretical space, to process everything that was happening.

Once they arrived, everyone climbed out—the men not as easily as the lassies—tentative smiles on their faces.

Again, she found herself doing a cursory glance for Dickie, but the street was empty except for a neighbor a few houses down sweeping her walkway.

"Wow, it's amazing how little things have changed in six years," Shona mused.

Moira's ears were immediately pricked. "Six? It's only been three."

Shona's brows raised and she looked frantically from Ewan to Rory. "Right, I forgot."

Moira's elation at seeing her sister quickly deflated. Was it possible to clone a body? Was this an automated robot made to look like Shona? She shook her head against all that scientific stuff and instead headed for the door.

Then, because she was feeling slightly paranoid, and a little concerned she might be delusional, she called out to her neighbor, "Afternoon, Mrs. MacArthur!"

"Hello, dear!" The elder woman stopped what she was doing. "Is that ye, Shona?"

So, Shona truly was standing behind her... Not delusional. She supposed she should consider that a win.

*Uh-oh*. The look on Mrs. MacArthur's face as she studied Moira's companions turned suspicious.

"It's so good to see ye again," Shona said.

"Ye, too, dearie. Where have ye been?" Mrs. MacArthur, holding a death grip on her broom, started to head toward them.

"Time to go inside," Rory said under his breath.

"We'll catch up again later," Shona called, hurrying in front of Moira. "Oh, wait, I don't have keys."

Moira tossed her sister the keys hoping she'd not forgotten how to unlock a door. Mrs. MacArthur looked positively intent on barreling forward. Shona unlocked the door and ducked inside with Moira ushering the two Highlanders inside before jogging up the steps herself, just as their nosy neighbor reached the end of their own private walkway.

"Pardon my manners, dear, but I couldn't help noticing your sister and her friend's state of dress. Where exactly has she been?"

Moira cocked her head, giving her neighbor a questioning, somewhat mind-your-own-business look. "State of dress?" She looked behind her into the house, all for show. "Their gym clothes?"

"Gym clothes?"

"Yes, gym clothes."

Mrs. MacArthur narrowed her brows.

"She takes appointments if ye're looking for a personal trainer. Well, gotta go! We haven't seen each other in forever." Moira didn't wait for her neighbor's response. Instead, she hurried through the door and slammed it shut.

But the moment she turned around, the room started to pulse in an out, as though some unseen force pressed in on her space. Her foyer started to fade. The faces of Rory, Shona and Ewan, too. What was happening? She put her arms out, bracing for a swoon. But she didn't feel faint. She felt... heavy. As though she wore a suit of rocks, holding her in place and pushing her down. Her vision blurred, and then the space around her turned black. She screamed, falling forward, and reaching out her hands to brace herself but not landing. From somewhere off in the distance she could hear Rory and Shona calling to her, telling her to remain calm. To breathe easy. How the hell did they expect her to breathe easy when the world around her had literally disappeared? Then she heard Shona's panicked words, muffled, and the soothing tones of Ewan as he tried to comfort her.

"What the hell is happening?" Moira cried. Was it an earthquake? Did a bomb rock their street? Oh, poor Mrs. MacArthur! Not even her broom could save her from this.

There was wind, like a tunnel. Birds. Then nothing. Then birds. Then nothing. Then wind and the rustling of... Were those trees? *Trees?*

They didn't sound at all like the small trees on her block... No, this rustling sounded like the great oaks of the Highlands where she liked to hike in the Cairngorms.

The blackness started to fade, and nausea kicked in as the world around her continued to pulse. Faster and faster. The world grew brighter. She felt like she was being birthed—as gross and weird as it was—as if she was being pushed from one world to the next. But that was impossible.

They must have drugged her. Must have done something. This was all a setup.

And then she was falling forward again, growing intense, and she had just enough time to brace herself as she landed in warm grass.

There were several thuds around her. She didn't waste time in scrambling to her feet, shoving off the ground as though it were on fire. Grass. Trees. Brush. She was in the woods. The bloody woods! She turned in a circle—okay, it was a clearing in the middle of the woods. No signs of civilization.

"What the fuck just happened?" she shouted, not one for cussing normally. But whateverthefuck just happened warranted a lot of fucking cussing!

Climbing to their feet around her, were Rory, Shona and Ewan. And none of them looked surprised. In fact, they each looked a little disappointed.

"I guess we just needed to come back to get ye," Rory said.

Anger spurred inside Moira. "Come back from where? Where the hell are we and—*what the fuck just happened?*" She was bordering on hysteria, and she knew it. But, if she was going to have a breakdown, there was no time like the present.

Maybe she should just lie on the grass, wait for whatever trippy drugs they'd given her to wear off.

Moira stared up at the late fall afternoon sky. Well... what should have been late fall. But the leaves were flourishing a brilliant green. And her face—the sun was warming it. The air around her was not as chilly as it should be, and actually, she was a little warm in her wool sweater dress and leather boots.

Just part of the dream. Summer was her favorite season. Her dreams would know that.

She sat down on the ground, the warmth of the grass

sinking all too real into her dark leggings. Tears started to sting her eyes, but she forced herself to swallow her fear. Crying wasn't going to help her. Not one bit. Plus, it would only show the others just how disturbed she was. And none of them seemed the least bit surprised at what had just happened.

Shona sank to the grass beside her, reaching for her hand. "Look, I know all of this must seem like some crazy nightmare, and ye're probably waiting to wake up, but this is real. I'm real."

Moira refused to look at her sister. Of course, the figment of Moira's imagination wanted her to believe all of this. But she refused. If she just sat here, not acknowledging the truth, then she would eventually come out of her drug-induced haze and face the world.

Or maybe she was having a mental breakdown. That could definitely be happening. The stress of it all taking its toll.

A sudden sting on her arm brought her momentarily back to the present. "Ouch!" Moira cried out staring at the spot of reddened skin where her sister pinched her. "Ye pinched me."

"Because, I wanted ye to know this *is* real."

Moira rubbed her arm. "I've felt pain in dreams before."

Shona sighed. "Fine, if this is all a dream, then it won't hurt ye to listen. To believe for a minute or two."

"I'm listening." Moira scowled. She couldn't help the attitude that spilled out in her tone.

She glanced at her sister, registering the hurt in Shona's expression.

Shona took a deep breath, keeping her gaze steadily locked on Moira's. "Hold my hand while I tell ye. Ye were always able to tell when I lied. Ye'll know I'm telling ye the truth."

Moira's only answer was to take her sister's hand.

"Before Ewan and I were in jail, we were here, in the Highlands, near Castle Gealach. But it wasn't... present day."

Moira's heart started to pound.

"It was 1544."

Again, Moira's vision started to blur. She let go of Shona's hand. *Ye will not pass out!* She chanted the words over and over in her head, clutched tight enough to her legs tucked up to her chest that she could feel the imprint of her nails on her shins. "1544?" she croaked. "As in the medieval times."

Shona nodded. "Just about. Technically the Renaissance era."

Her sister held up her hands in surrender when Moira was about to protest at her issue with the wording.

"What ye're telling me is that there is such a thing as time-travel?" Her head fell back and she stared up once more at the swaying tree branches, feeling the warmth of summer breeze on her skin. Seemed like all that science-y stuff that she'd feared earlier was actually the explanation they were going to toss her way. "And I'm supposed to believe that the three of ye are time-travelers."

Shona nodded. "I know it's a lot to take in. I could barely grasp it myself, but as soon as we landed in the park—naked I might add—my memory was fully restored." Shona glanced at Ewan.

"Ewan, ye're taking this rather well," Rory said.

"Aye." Ewan raised a brow, an obvious challenge to get him to say more.

"How?" Rory asked him.

Moira found herself keenly interested in whatever answer he could come up with, especially if it meant she didn't have to say anything.

"This was not my first time," Ewan murmured.

"Nay?" Rory said.

Ewan shook his head. "I first traveled to Gealach many

years ago. I was an adolescent at the time, taken in by the folks at the castle when I landed on the shore—though I didna remember until arriving in Edinburgh, with Shona, that it was a plane crash that brought me to the past. And—" He swiped his hand over his face. "Fuck me... 'Tis no wonder Lady Emma kept saying I reminded her of someone. I'm her brother. And it explains Rory's sudden disappearance, the man would never have been found."

"Bloody hell," Rory said. "That's a long time to go without knowing who ye are. Brother to Lady Emma wife of the Guardian?"

Ewan nodded.

Who was Lady Emma?

This all felt like a dream as Moira's gaze swiveled in slow motion from one to the next of them. "Um, hey, so this is my first time here, and I don't know Lady Emma or the Guardian," she started. "And I'm kinda feeling in the dark."

"Ohmygod..." Shona said, shaking her head, seeming to ignore Moira. "I knew Emma was a time-traveler. But ye, Ewan, I had no idea, why didn't ye tell me? We've shared everything."

"I thought it was enough when we were in Saughton to let ye know I'd not traveled before. Ye were in such a panic."

"Why would time make us forget? So we could cope with our new world?" Shona asked no one in particular. "That wouldn't make sense, because Rory and Moira both have never forgotten."

"I suppose, it was necessary until time was ready for us to once more travel." Ewan yanked a fallen limb the rest of the way off a tree and began breaking off the tiny branches that covered it.

Shona dropped her face into her hands. "This is my fault. The moon, the herbs, the stone."

"But, we've found Rory and your sister," Ewan offered, dropping the branch and coming to rest his hand on her back.

"Hello?" Moira waved her hand feeling as though she were completely invisible. "I'm so completely lost right now guys."

Rory settled down beside her, tried to put his arm around her, and even though she knew it was simply to comfort her, she shrugged him off. He took the hint, but didn't stray from his seat next to her. The sad thing was, she *did* want his comfort, she just couldn't make herself take it.

"I need a drink," she murmured.

"I think I can help with that," Ewan said. "There's a tavern around here that I've visited afore. We'll need to get off the road, besides."

Shona groaned. "Not *that* tavern."

Ewan wiggled his brows wickedly pricking Moira's curiosity all the more. This dream, or hallucination, or even reality, whatever it was, was pretty interesting. Perhaps if she just went with it, continued to follow these apparitions around, she'd eventually wake up and have a good laugh at her overactive imagination. What was that old saying? *If ye can't beat 'em, join 'em.*

"I want to know what *that tavern* means," Moira teased, shocking everyone present.

Ewan was the first to recover. "Ah-ha, ye're much like your sister. Let us go then, and be entertained."

"I refuse to be entertained," Shona said sarcastically, then leaned toward Moira. "It's a brothel more than it is a tavern."

A real, live, historical brothel? Oh, now this was getting good. "Take me there. I insist," Moira said rather jovially.

Again, there was silence for a moment or two, and each of the three stared at her with blank expressions. Was this when she'd wake up? Was this when the room would finally reappear around her and she'd hear her alarm waking her up for her run with Dickie? Well, if it was, then she would cancel on him. If anything, this wicked dream had taught her a thing or two, one of which was he was not the right guy for her.

"Well?" she said, climbing to her feet and holding out her arms in exaggerated exasperation. "I'm ready to get the party started."

Shona stood, too, and pressed the back of her hand to Moira's forehead. "Are ye certain ye're feeling all right?"

"Never better." She beamed a smile at Rory. "What say ye, Highlander, should ye like to dally at the tavern?"

That made Rory come close to peer into her eyes and check her for fever, too. "She's in shock," he said.

"Aye," Ewan agreed. "A walk through the woods and a stiff whisky ought to help. 'Haps a nap while we figure out what day it is, and if the word is out that we're missing. And ye—" He pointed at Rory. "We need to get ye off the road. There are many people searching for ye."

Moira's gut clenched. This didn't sound good.

"Aye. Henchmen, too." Shona shivered.

Moira did the same. *This isn't real. This isn't real.*

"Dammit." Rory studied the woods around him as if expecting one of the henchmen to make himself known, then he, too, yanked on a fallen limb to create a walking stick.

"What happened?" Shona asked. "I know ye didn't do what they've been saying ye did."

"What are they saying?" Rory asked.

"Murder. Betrayal." Ewan's gaze was steady on Rory, his eyes assessing and Moira got the sense that if he'd been born in present day—well, if he'd *stayed* in present day—he would have been a great addition to MI6.

"They're wrong about murder. I've never killed anyone who didna need killing."

"That's not exactly a good answer." Shona rolled her eyes.

"Battle, lass."

"And betrayal?" Moira said, her eyes welling with tears. She bit the inside of her cheek, fearing the answer.

Rory seemed to struggle for the words, the muscles in his jaw clenching and a vein beginning to throb in his neck.

"We'll discuss it more at the tavern, away from the road," Ewan said. "If anyone sees us, he'll be recognized."

They all agreed without consulting Moira, not that she expected them to; in fact, she ignored them, her mind reaching and failing to grasp the newness of her reality. Whatever her little ghostlike friends wanted to say was fine by her. She'd changed her entire attitude about this situation. She was here for the fun of it until she woke up. Hell, already she'd learned she wanted to break up with her boyfriend. Maybe she'd learn a thing or two more about herself before the dream was over.

They started toward the woods with Ewan saying he was pretty certain he knew where the road was from the glen. Moira shook her head. Definitely a dream, because not one of them questioned his sense of direction in a circle of land where all the trees looked the same.

As they walked, Shona talked more, rambling on, with barely a breath drawn, and Moira listened, nodding, as she was certain she was supposed to do. "...Rory had been missing for two years. It was hard to move on without him, but I fell in love. We wanted to have a child. We went out to a clearing, where there is a magical stone, and we began to... pray. Ye see, at the time, I didn't know exactly who I was. I couldn't remember much of anything other than how Rory had helped me settle here. As far as I'd always known, I was from the Highlands, born in the 1500's, except for these flashes of memory. Over the years, I became half-certain that I had somehow come from another place, and half-certain I was going mad. When Rory disappeared, I made do on my own, odd healing jobs for people in need, and eventually made it all the way to the castle as a healer. I suppose, our little tea and spice shop helped with the knowledge I had. I'd spent the last five or six years thinking I was a trained healer by trade. That perhaps I'd come from a family of healers. Can ye imagine? I mean, maybe we do. Perhaps somewhere down the long line, the Ayreshires were great healers. Maybe even wizards."

Ewan stopped suddenly in his tracks, probably because he was lost. His face had paled.

But the question he asked next had Moira once more trying to pinch herself awake.

"Did ye say Ayreshire? As in the Earls of Carrick? As in Turnberry Castle, as in descendants of Robert the Bruce?"

## 9

RORY

"What are ye saying?" Rory asked. Forget the danger of henchmen looking for him; the fear for Shona and Moira in Ewan's eyes was enough to raise the hair on the back of his neck.

Though he'd never met Ewan before, he'd heard of the man plenty. Tales of his prowess on the battlefield as well as with the lassies were heard all over the Highlands—though Rory was pleased to see he'd settled down with Shona, and was no longer pursuing his female conquests.

Ewan was second-in-command to Laird Logan Grant, Guardian of Scotland and protector of Castle Gealach. And though there was a price on Rory's head, he thought he could trust this man.

"I'm not saying anything yet," Ewan said, hands on his hips as he stared at the ground in thought, then he glanced back up at Rory. "Do ye know the tale?"

He gave a curt shake of his head. "Not all. Tell it."

"We need to keep moving," Ewan said. "I'll tell it over whisky, after ye explain the accusations against ye."

Nobody argued, especially not Rory, because bits and

pieces of a tale he'd heard as a child were coming to his memory, and if what he recalled had an ounce of truth, then... Well, he didn't want to contemplate the gravity of their current situation.

At all.

Moira slipped her hand into his. "Isn't this a lovely jaunt?" she asked.

Rory frowned. "Ye're not acting yourself, lass. What's wrong?"

She leaned her head against his shoulder as they walked, but it didn't feel genuine. "Why should there be anything wrong?"

"Because a quarter hour ago ye were screaming obscenities. Now, ye seem as chipper as a drunk lass on May Day."

"What's May Day?"

"Come now, ye know what May Day is."

"Oh, right. We celebrated that with a bonfire didn't we? And ye tried to get me to dance naked around the flames."

Rory chuckled. "Almost had ye, too."

Her head snapped off his shoulder. "Well, I guess I can tell ye." She waved her hands in the air. "This is all a dream, so I'm going with it."

"Going with it?" he questioned. The phrase was not familiar to him.

"Yes. I'm playing along." Her smile was vibrant, but her eyes were dazed.

Rory was worried about her. She was truly in shock. "Lass, this is no game. Ye and your sister could be in grave danger."

That made her laugh. "Let me guess, there are bandits in these woods."

"Aye."

"And wild animals that would want to shred me to bits."

"Right again."

"Oh, stop it. Let's go get drunk."

Rory stopped moving. Hands on her shoulders he forced her to look at him. "This is no dream, lass. And if ye refuse to believe me, then at least pretend to take caution. My time... it is not as ordered as yours."

Her smile faltered, eyes shuttered. "Ordered?"

"Ye have police that can come at the drop of a hat. Ye have shelters and things like electricity, showers, and hospitals. We've not got that here."

Her face paled, and she looked ready to faint again. "Nay, nay, nay," he said hurriedly. "Ye're not going to do that again."

"Rory?"

"Aye, love?"

"Why is this happening?" Her voice sounded so small, and he wanted nothing more than to wrap her up in his arms and protect her forever.

"I dinna know. But we'll find out."

"I want to go home now. This isn't fun."

"Lass, I think ye are home."

She glanced around. "I would feel like I was home if I was." She shook her head. "And I don't."

Rory pressed a kiss to her forehead and pulled her into his arms. She sank against him, her fingers digging into his shirt as though she'd find anchor for the rest of time. He was more than happy to be that anchor.

For years, he'd been an outsider, not one to belong. It was only when he was with Moira that he felt at home—in this time or hers. As long as she was by his side, he knew he was on the right path.

"Damn," Ewan said, stiffening at the same time Rory heard the crunch of footsteps through the woods.

"We're not alone," Rory said.

"And neither of us with a weapon, unless ye count this." Ewan held up the walking stick he'd prepared himself. "I assume ye can fight." Ewan gave him an assessing glance.

"Used to be the captain of the guard for my laird," Rory said—until his laird's castle and lands were seized, the entire clan massacred and Rory decided to take a vow of solitude, which led him to Moira. "We'll have to fight with our staffs."

"I can fight," Shona said. "I've done it before." Then she winked at Ewan.

"Nay, not this time, love," Ewan said, pulling her in for a quick kiss.

Seeing that moment of affection made Rory wish he and Moira were as close. They'd get there again. He vowed it. For now, he settled on kissing the top of her stubborn head.

Shona rushed over to Moira and grabbed her hand. "Come on, we need to get up this tree and hide."

"Up the tree?" Moira looked baffled. "No way. I'm ready to wake up now. I'm ready."

"Shh!" Shona hissed. "They'll hear ye, and we've got to keep hidden."

Fire filled Moira's eyes and for the first time since they'd landed back in his time, Rory started to see the return of some of the backbone he knew Moira possessed.

"Fine. But I'm going to need more than whisky after this. I want a turkey leg, too."

"Aye." Rory chuckled, though his skin was prickling as he heard whoever stalked the woods getting closer. "I'll give ye a boost, and when we're through, I'll get ye whatever ye want." Effortlessly he picked her up, thrilling at the feel of her lush legs on his palms. "Grab hold of that tree limb and swing yourself up."

She did as he instructed, scrambling up into the foliage, then stood on the limb to reach for a higher one.

Rory was about to ask if she should do that when Shona said, "She was great at climbing trees as a kid. And she did gymnastics, great on the high bars. Anyways, I suspect it's a skill she's not lost."

Shona effortlessly swung herself up into the tree—obviously a skill that both twins possessed, but Rory had no more time to think on it. Not a second after the lassies disappeared, a grungy-looking trio of men pushed through the thorn bushes, not seeming to care the least for the barbs that snagged their clothes.

They stopped short, but the stench of them did not. Rory's eyes almost watered. They smelled of piss, ale and a year or two's worth of filth.

"*Sassenachs*," the shortest of the three hissed, spittle falling from his lips.

"Hate to disappoint ye, mate," Rory said. "But we're Scots through and through."

"Why ye dressed like that then?"

Dammit. He glanced down at his denim pants and cotton shirt. Ewan was still in his prison garb.

Rory shrugged. "Helps us blend in."

The men screwed up their faces as though he'd said he was a mermaid in disguise. Rory loved to harass with imbeciles. The trio of buffoons didn't say anything to that, and several very tense moments passed between them all as Rory studied their weapons, clothes and anything they might have hidden beneath. He and Ewan could easily overtake them, but he'd not even accept a thousand gold coins to wear their filthy, lice-riddled clothes. Not on his life. Well, maybe if his life was in danger, but it wasn't yet.

"What are ye doing in our territory?" the man in the center, perhaps their leader, if there was one, said, then burped loudly and bent over as though he might retch.

"Your territory?" Rory asked, grimacing in disgust. "Are ye the laird?" His tone was filled with sarcasm.

The leader pulled his sword from the scabbard at his hip and stabbed the tip into the ground, then leaned on it for balance. "So what if I am? Ye'll have to pay a tax to get around me."

"How would ye like us to pay?" Rory glanced at Ewan who was nonchalantly spinning the tip of his staff in the ground.

"Well, that's easy. Give us all your coin."

"We dinna have any coin," Rory answered. "Think ye, if we had coin, we'd be dressed like this?"

"I knew ye didna want to dress like that! I knew it. Ye dinna blend in at all," the short one said, nodding and smiling as though he'd figured out some grand scheme all on his own.

"Right," Rory said. "Ye figured us out."

"And if he was lying about that, then he's probably lying about the coin," the third one, tall and thin as a whipping pole, spilled out to the short one, even going so far as to lean behind the leader's back.

"Ye know we can hear ye?" Ewan asked, shaking his head in revulsion. "Rory, I think we should just put these blokes out of their misery."

"A good plan."

The leader laughed. "But we've got swords and ye've got naught but a bunch of sticks and tight hose on your legs."

"Well, then we'll just have to relieve ye of your weapons," Rory said. "Or beat ye with our sticks and strangle ye with our hose."

Rory tossed his staff, twirling it in the air before catching it and arching it toward the ground hard and fast enough that they felt the air rush against their faces.

"What the—" the short one said, cutting himself off and backing up.

"Stay, we'll have a good time." Rory grinned like a madman.

"Aye, we will. Ye'll not beat me with your wood," the leader growled, pulling his sword from the ground and wavering on his feet."

"This seems most unfair," Ewan laughed.

"Aye. The man can barely stand. I've an idea," Rory said to the maggot. "Why dinna ye knock yourself to the ground so I dinna have to?"

That only made the man growl, and he ran at Rory, sword outstretched. Rory shook his head. What was the world coming to? He stepped aside and the man kept going, stumbling forward, his sword stabbing into the tree where the lassies hid.

Rory waited as the man tried to yank his sword free. Ewan had already dispatched of the willowy outlaw, who lay in slumber, a knot on his forehead, and the short one was ready to piss himself. He dropped to his knees and held his hands up in surrender.

The leader finally yanked his sword free, but when he turned around, he did so right into the end of Rory's staff and crumpled to the ground.

"When I said knock yourself out, I had no idea ye'd actually go through with it," he muttered to the unconscious man.

"This was, without a doubt, the worst fight I've ever had," Ewan said. "Bloody disappointing."

"I'm sorry, sir, meant no harm, sir," the little one was babbling.

Rory rolled his eyes in disgust. "Do ye have a rope?" he asked the fool.

"Aye."

"Give it to me."

The man tugged off a satchel he had at his back and pulled out a rope. "Here ye go."

With a deep sigh, Rory used the man's rope to tie him and his two companions up. "Dinna prey on those who appear weak, for ye never know when ye may have chosen wrong."

"Aye, sir. Please, I beg ye, dinna kill me, sir."

"Now why would I go to the trouble I tying ye up, if I meant to kill ye?"

"Good point, sir."

"Shut your filthy mouth," Ewan growled. "I'm done hearing it, and your breath is wicked foul."

The men taken care of, Rory returned to the tree to see the lassies were already climbing down, humor in their eyes.

"Jump, I'll catch ye," Ewan said to Shona.

Rory watched with envy as she jumped without hesitation. Moira was nimbly climbing down with a glare on her face that said if he dared to ask her to jump, she'd jump and then kick him in the ballocks.

"Ye've a talent I knew nothing of," he said.

"Ye dinna know everything about me," she retorted.

"This is true. 'Twould be a pleasure to learn more of your secrets."

Moira grunted. "Well, that was rather pathetic." She put her hands on her hips and glared down at the men on the ground. "Is that how most of your fights go?"

Rory's expression grew serious. "That was a first like that and hopefully the last."

"Shall we be on our way, then?" Ewan asked. "We've got at least another hour or two before we reach the tavern, and I can hear Shona's belly grumbling."

Shona playfully slapped her lover's arm.

"I'm getting hungry, too," Moira mumbled, pressing her hand to her belly. "That's odd. I've never been hungry in a dream before. I've been eating. I've been cooking. But never actually hungry."

Rory slipped his hand in hers. "Ye're not dreaming, love."

This was the second time he called her love, and she didn't tell him not to. Perhaps it was because she was thinking too deeply, but he'd take it as a couple stones removed from the wall she'd built around herself.

They divested the three outlaws of the little bit of coin they possessed and their weapons.

"The tavern should have a few extra plaids, some shirts and gowns for us all to change into. They get enough men leaving stuff behind," Ewan said.

"Running out of the place from angry husbands?" Moira asked.

"Or Hildie. She's one angry mistress," Ewan said.

"She is not going to be happy to see ye," Shona said to Ewan.

"Oh, I dinna know about that." Ewan winked.

"Don't say its because she really liked ye," Shona warned.

Ewan laughed. "Well, she did."

Shona growled, and he tickled her ribs. "Relax, love. She's not going to try to seduce me. Hildie might be jealous of ye, but she always did want me to find my way."

"And have ye?"

"I have."

Pangs of envy again assaulted Rory. Lord, how badly he wanted to have such banter with Moira. They did once. At one point, he'd been certain they would be together forever, that the fates had brought them together because they were meant to be. Hell, what was he thinking? He *still* felt that way. Somehow, he had to show her that she could trust him again.

"I know this is a lot to take in," he said softly. "But I promise I'll be here to take care of ye every step of the way. Fate brought us together. Fate brought me to ye twice now."

"Is this the part where ye say that it's Fate we should be together again?" Moira said skeptically. "Because I don't believe in Fate, Rory. I believe in forging my own path. Long before ye came around, Shona and I had to fend for ourselves. We had to make our own path and now it just sort of feels like it's all crumbling apart."

"I know what that feels like." Again, he remembered the massacre. Being alone in the center of a bloody battlefield.

"How?"

"Before I came to ye the first time, I failed my entire clan. We were besieged. I was the captain of the guard, lead warrior." He shook his head. "My laird was taken. His wife, too. Their people slaughtered, and it was all I could do to hack at one man after another while a few of the people escaped."

"Where are they now?"

"Dead." A familiar pain in his chest pulsed. "I chased after the men who took them. We fought. They left me for dead. When I came to, my mistress and my laird lay dead beside me. 'Twas my fault. I wanted to save them, but in the end, I got them killed. I stumbled back toward the castle, but I was too injured to make it. I found an abandoned croft. I tended my own wounds, and fell into a fever amongst the ruins. Days, maybe weeks passed, I dinna know, but when I tried to leave the croft, I ended up outside your spice shop."

"I remember that day. Ye were pretty sick." Moira's tender gaze stroked over him.

"Aye. Somehow, Fate brought me to ye, so ye could save me. And I think it was because I was meant to save ye."

## ❧ 10 ❧

### MOIRA

All the talk of fate was starting to give Moira a headache. Well, more specifically, her rumbling belly and the stress of traveling back in time five hundred years. Yes, she'd come to the conclusion, as harebrained as it was, that she must have actually traveled through time. How else could she explain the rumbling in her belly and the cramping in her limbs from all the walking? Besides her cup of coffee that morning, she'd not eaten breakfast or lunch, and soon it would be dinner.

"Fate," she whispered.

"Aye."

She was glad that Rory was with her. Relieved that her sister was okay. Even more comforted by the knowledge that the two of them hadn't run off together.

"There is so much I need to learn." Though she'd said it aloud, the thought was more internal. She didn't just need to learn about this historical place she'd been tossed, but she needed to know where she was headed, and how the hell to get back to present day. She had a shop to run, a house.

People who counted on her. "So, there wasn't an earthquake or a bomb that shook our street?"

She glanced sideways at Rory, seeing his grave expression, honest eyes.

"Nay, lass. Unfortunately, traveling through time can kind of feel like that, but it isn't. Mrs. MacArthur should be safe at home, peering through her curtains and spying on the people walking around outside."

Moira smiled. "She'll be the first one to report me missing."

"No doubt, and how ye were swept off by your wayward sister who must have just escaped from Saughton Prison."

Moira shook her head, still trying to wrap her mind around everything. She was struggling, but... "It just doesn't feel real."

"I know how ye feel. The first time it happened to me, I was certain I'd died and gone to the afterlife."

"Heaven or Hell?"

"Depends on my mood," he chuckled. "Every moment with ye was like being in Heaven. Every moment in these damn denim was like being in Hell."

"Ye don't have to flatter me so much," Moira said, realizing, as the words came out, that she sounded a little bitchy, unappreciative. He'd just offered her a compliment and she stomped on it. "I'm sorry. I... it's been such a long day, and I'm getting a little hangry."

"Hangry?"

"Hungry, angry."

"Huh." He looked mystified, rolling the syllables on his tongue. "Hangry. What about hunfrustgry?"

"What?" She looked up at him, not sure she heard him right.

He shrugged. "Hungry, frustrated, angry. If ye can make up words, so can I."

That made her laugh out loud, perhaps the first genuine laugh of the day. "I didn't make up hangry. They're going to add it to the dictionary if they haven't already. Kind of like selfie."

"What are ye talking about?" Shona and Ewan slowed down so they could walk beside them.

"Your sister is hunfrustgry." Rory smirked when he said it.

"That's odd," Shona said, furrowing her brow. "What does it mean?"

Moira rolled her eyes. "I'm hungry, frustrated, a little angry."

"Oh." Shona's expression dropped and she put her arm around Moira's shoulder. "I'm sorry."

"There is no need for ye to be sorry. Ye cannot stop Fate, and ye're not the first in our group to time travel," Moira said.

"Ah, the first, that would be me, so then, I'm sorry," Ewan said, though there was humor in his voice.

"I don't blame ye either," Moira said.

A light breeze whistled through the trees. The air was so fresh. So clean. She'd been up north many times in present day, and always thought the air was easier to breathe—but now, it seemed even smoother. Industrialization had yet to come to anyplace on earth, the land was still untouched by pollution.

"Is that water I hear?" Moira asked, cocking her head. Her tongue was dry, and her stomach rumbled again.

Somewhere off to the right, she could have sworn she heard the sounds of water trickling.

"I think so," Rory said.

They headed to the right, stepping over logs, and for the first time Moira actually looked at every tree. The bark, the sage-colored lichen spreading over trunks and the moss that sprouted on rocks jutting from the earth. They'd not yet reached whatever road Ewan was taking them toward, and this part of the world seemed as though it could have been completely untouched by human hands.

Birds flew from tree to tree overhead, settling on branches and cocking their heads at the four intruders into their peaceful domain. Squirrels darted this way and that, climbing in circular patterns up the trees. Tiny white, purple and pink flowers sprouted randomly in places, some on bushes, others on vines that wove their own paths on the forest floors.

Nature was alive in this place, a time of its own, and a beauty that was eternal. From somewhere deep within her Moira felt a tugging of hidden emotion. Was it pride? The sense of feeling like she'd come home? Her limbs seemed to speak to the earth around her, and she felt pulled, drawn. She'd never felt it before. It was almost euphoric in a sense. Happiness, pure and simple.

And that made no sense. Happiness should be the furthest thing from her mind.

*Why shouldn't I be happy?* She stood between the two most important people in her own world. The people she loved. The people she wanted to spend time with every single day.

Moira breathed in deep. At least, if she was going to travel back in time she came to a place that was beautiful, with the, people she cared most about in the world. She supposed she should be grateful for the favors Fate or the time-space-continuum had deemed to give her.

"I'm the one who is sorry," she said softly, glancing first at her sister, meeting her eyes and then to Rory. "I didn't understand what was happening, what happened to you in the past, and I still haven't fully grasped it all, but I should have tried harder from the beginning. I'm sorry. I've been acting like, kind of an arsehole, all day. I promise to do better."

Shona squeezed her shoulders, and Rory clutched her fingers a little tighter.

"We've all been there. Trust us, we won't hold any of your reactions against ye," Shona said. "I'm just so damned glad to have my memory back! I know where I came from. I can't believe I spent five years not knowing who ye were."

"Shite. I just thought of something," Rory broke in as the trickling stream came into view.

"What is it?" Moira asked, feeling panic tighten hold around her ribs.

"We dinna know what year it is."

"We just assumed we were back in our time," Ewan said.

"Aye, but the truth is, I came from 1541 to see Moira, and ye both came from 1544."

"*Mo chreach*," Ewan muttered.

"That means, we dinna even know *if* the king lives," Shona said.

"What do ye mean, if he lives?" Rory asked.

"He died of an ague last December. His daughter born just days before. She was crowned queen when she was nine months old."

"Mary Queen of Scots," Moira said. Something she knew about history. "England is at constant war with Scotland."

They all nodded.

Moira, feeling her fingers grow tingly and her legs weak, dropped down with the pretense of sipping some water. The woods were full of more dangers than just a few drunken outlaws. The English could be roaming anywhere and all they had were the rusty weapons of the outlaws they'd essentially robbed.

The water was cool on her fingertips and she brought it to her mouth, sipping. The chill liquid forged a path all the way to her belly, and eased some of the rumbling. She splashed water on her face, rubbed some around the back of her neck.

"We are in somewhat better shape in 1541 than 1544," Shona said.

"Why's that?" Rory asked.

"Because in 1544, there is much unrest. Castle Gealach is even more dangerous now with an infant princess on the throne. The treasure of Gealach and the crown itself are much sought after. Then again, Henry VIII has proposed a marriage between the infant queen and his son, so I suppose the English aren't roaming as much," Shona said with a shrug.

"We have to find out. What if we fell even further back in time and William Wallace is still leading the Scottish armies and Longshanks is ready to ride through these woods at any moment?" Moira dipped her hands into the creek, sucking down more water after the words fell from her lips.

"That would be bad." Rory kicked at a rock in the earth, and when it came slightly free, bent to pick it up. He tossed it toward the water, and she watched it skip once, twice, three times. "We should tell them, Ewan. Tell them about the Ayreshire lassies."

"Tell us what?" Moira asked.

"Depends on the year," Ewan said.

"Tell us!" Shona said, marching over to Ewan and pinching his arm.

"Ow," Ewan said, though it was obvious from the crinkle of humor around his eyes, he felt no pain. "All right, I'll tell ye. Ye might as well know the danger."

"Ohmygod, more danger." Moira's breath hitched. *Just what I need...*

"The story goes, the Ayreshire girls were the legitimate heirs to the Scottish throne through their father King David II of Scotland, son of Robert the Bruce. Their birth was never recorded as their father was imprisoned in England at the time they were conceived. The queen was allowed to visit him a few times."

"Why wouldn't she tell anyone she was pregnant or that she gave birth?" Shona asked.

Ewan shrugged. "Maybe since her husband was imprisoned for so many years by the enemy, their children's lives were in danger?"

"That means..." Moira's mouth was suddenly dry once more.

"We could be queen." Shona paled, her hand coming to her throat as if she already imagined being beheaded.

"Nay, not both of ye," Rory said. "Only one of ye."

"Twins again..." Shona whispered.

"What?" Moira and Rory said in unison.

Ewan remained silent.

Shona licked her lips and shook her head. "Nothing. Just a rumor I heard. Something about Laird Grant being the twin brother of the king."

"The late king," Rory said.

"Or maybe he's still the present king," Ewan uttered.

"Or maybe he's not even born yet," Moira mused.

"We need to find out what year it is. Everything hinges on that." Ewan wiped the water from his face with this shirt.

"I need a drink, and not the water kind." Rory reached down his hand to Moira where she'd sunk again by the water's edge. "How are ye holding up?"

She reached for his hand, glad for the warmth and strength he exuded. "I've been better."

"If we've made it back to our own time, the tavern should only be another half-hour or so from here. If not... well, the place has been there for a long time. People have been drinking, eating and whor—" Ewan cut himself short. "Enjoying themselves, for many years."

EWAN

JUST AS EWAN PREDICTED, THE TAVERN WAS ONLY A SHORT distance away. They'd been walking for hours, and considering she was in her thick, fall boots, not made for hiking, Moira's feet were hot and killing her.

A dozen or so yards away, the tavern loomed from the ground up. A stone and wooden building that looked a lot more like a historical house than it did a tavern. A few horses were tied up inside a makeshift stable. The scents of horse manure, garbage and roasted chicken filled the air. The latter of which didn't seem at all appetizing with the two afore mentioned scents.

Laughter echoed in the small glen that housed the tavern. It seemed like a jovial establishment.

"I suppose only one of us should venture forth." Ewan frowned, scanning the building. "Wish I could remember what sort of foliage Hildie had planted around the front of the place. There looks to be a small garden and a few fruit trees. But I canna honestly remember if they were here before."

"Ye go first then," Shona teased. "Besides, if Hildie does recognize ye, then we'll have no need to worry."

Ewan grinned. "I think this might be the first time ye've ever been glad for another woman to recognize me."

"Oh, its not the recognizing that's ever bothered me, love," Shona teased. "It's the, *Oh, Ewan, remember when we...*" Shona sang softly and sweetly as she swaggered in a small circle around her lover.

They all laughed behind their hands, trying to keep the sounds from carrying.

"Shona." Ewan cleared his throat and he tugged her abruptly out of sight behind some trees leaving Moira and Rory alone.

Moira's breath hitched, a little with fear and trepidation.

What was going to happen next? They had no clue as far as the scale of what sort of shit they were about to fall into.

"I know I've said it at least a dozen times in the last hour, but I'll keep ye safe, Moira. Ye have my word." Rory's voice was soft and filled with conviction.

She studied his handsome face, her eyes roving over his chiseled features, his hair the color of night, none of the red showing in the shade. Out of instinct, she reached up and touched his cheek, the stubble tickling her palm.

"I know. And I trust ye."

He let out a breath, taking a step closer. He brushed her cheek with the backs of his fingers. "Ye're still as beautiful as I remember. I missed ye so much."

Emotion swelled inside her. "I missed ye, too." Her body acted before the thought had a chance to cement itself, and she was closing the distance between them. *She* was leaning up on tiptoe. *She* was grabbing hold of his waist and tugging him forward. *She* was pressing her lips to his.

Moira needed this. Needed to melt into his kiss. Needed this world, the next, and whatever else lay between, to melt away.

God help her, but she still loved him.

## 🕈 11 🕈
### SHONA

"Shona..." Ewan pressed his forehead to hers, his hands cupping the sides of her face.

Shona closed her eyes. There was no predicting what would happen once her husband ducked under the threshold of the tavern. There was no guessing at whether those within would help, or harm.

"Be safe," she whispered, and, "I love ye," because there was nothing else she could say. Nothing else she wanted him to think about when he was walking into a potential trap.

"I will, *mo chridhe*." And then he kissed her, pressing his lips to hers with such passion, such fervor that she felt it all the way to her toes. "I love ye so much," he murmured, never taking his mouth from hers.

She hated what this heated kiss represented. A possible goodbye, for she knew that was what it was. His tongue swept over hers in arcs and she worked to memorize every line of his body with her hands as though she hadn't already.

Flames of desire, of need, of desperation engulfed her.

"Ye'd better come back to me."

"I will fight until the end to be at your side."

The drunken outlaws who had attacked them before were no match, no threat even, and they were nothing compared to what she'd seen. What she herself had done in the past. She'd killed a man who endangered her life and Ewan's, leaving her husband for dead. But she'd healed many more. She had a place here, a purpose, unlike back in present day where she felt like she aimlessly walked the streets searching for the meaning of life. Her only solace had been the company of her sister, the mixing of herbs in their spice shop. Even back then—or before? How did one differentiate?—she had a gift for herbs and healing, and many loyal customers. They likely missed her, but there were others, there were hospitals. Not here. The doctors were just as likely to kill a person in the 1500's than provide succor. Here, *she* could really help.

There was no doubt where she wanted to be. And thank goodness her sister was now with her, too.

But Ewan... He was her whole life! Without him, even the mixing of her herbs would hold no appeal. She'd not be able to save anyone if she couldn't save herself, and if something happened to him—well, then she'd be lost, devastated, life would cease to exist.

Shona clung to him. They'd not been married long. About a year, and yet so much had happened.

The MacDonalds still lay low, an occasional raid to keep the Grants on their toes. Emma had admitted that she was a time-traveler, had told Shona all about her and Logan's love. So deep and intense. The same as what she felt for Ewan.

She could have stayed here, hiding behind a thick oak, kissing her husband, until the end of time, but she knew they couldn't. With one last, long, deep kiss, she pulled regrettably away from him.

"Go now, before I tie ye to this tree." The words hurt

coming out. How could she tell him to leave her? To willingly walk into danger.

"How about I tie ye to the tree when I come back?" he murmured against her ear. "I'll pleasure ye for hours and ye'll not be able to escape my touch."

"I will hold ye to that promise."

Ewan's smile was wicked and filled his face. Even his eyes twinkled. "I knew I married the perfect lass, but each day that passes shows me even more just how right I was."

"And ye'd best remember it walking into Hildie's Tavern..."

Ewan chuckled, tweaking her chin. "Jealous?" But before she could answer, he swooped down and kissed her hard once more. "Ye're the only woman I want. I love ye."

"I love ye, too. Now go."

Ewan nodded curtly, taking her hand and leading her back to her sister and Rory. They stopped short when they happened upon the other two in an embrace. Shona had known Rory for years, and before he'd disappeared, he'd not once entertained a woman. Now she knew why. All the time that had passed seemed not to have lessened Moira's and his affection for one another.

Ewan purposefully stepped on a fallen stick, snapping it to pull the two of them from their embrace, but that didn't work. They'd not even seemed to hear it. Their passion clouded all their senses it would seem, or else they were ignoring them.

Ewan cleared his throat.

That didn't work either.

"Saints, but they must be really into it," Ewan muttered.

"There's been several times the two of us have felt the same." She leaned against him.

"Aye, but we've work to do."

"Truth." Shona cleared her throat and then sang out softly, "Moira."

That seemed to get their attention. They finally broke apart, her sister's face completely flushed.

"I'm going in." Ewan kept his gaze on Rory. "If I'm not back in five minutes, take the women to safety."

"My cottage."

"Aye. If for some reason I am waylaid, I will meet ye there."

Rory nodded.

Shona couldn't let go of Ewan's hand. "Be careful," she said.

"I always am."

And then his hand was slipping from hers and he was walking with confident strides toward the front door of the tavern. Without saying anything, Moira came to stand beside Shona, her hand slipping against her sister's, silent comfort.

From their place in the woods, they were hidden from sight of anyone inside the tavern who peered out a window, but they had a good view of the front door of the building. Ewan reached a hand to knock when the door was flung wide. A long, slender arm stretched out, grabbed onto his and tugged him inside, quickly slamming the door shut. On instinct, Shona lurched forward, ready to go investigate where exactly her husband had just gone and with whom, but Moira held her back.

"No," Moira whispered.

"The countdown begins," Rory mumbled.

The minutes ticked by like an eternity. None of them spoke. The air vibrated from their nerves. What was taking so long? Was that Hildie's arm? Was Ewan safe?

## EWAN

"What are ye doing here?" Hildie hissed.

Ewan didn't know whether to be relieved that Hildie looked exactly the same, or worried at her panicked tone and shifty eyes. She tugged him to the left of the door into a private dining room and away from the main barroom, shutting the door behind her.

"I need your help," he said. "What's happened?"

"Everyone knows ye've gone missing and Logan has declared war on the MacDonalds—who by the way seem to think your wife is something pretty special, or that she knows something that could help MacDonald's cause."

Ewan prayed it had something to do with Rory, or even Shona's skill, and nothing to do with her bloodline.

"I need to ask ye an odd question."

"Honey, nothing could phase me in this place. Ye wouldn't believe the things I've heard."

"How long have I been missing?"

"We need to get ye out of here. Ye've been missing for going on two months."

Ewan glanced around the room, taking in the familiar setting. A small round table with several chairs. A stained tablecloth. Candles. Jugs of wine and whisky on the sideboard. "Why do ye need to get me out of here?"

Hildie looked behind her at the closed door, and held her finger to her lips. Ewan strained to hear what she heard, but other than the commotion from the men drinking beyond, the creaking of the floorboards above his head, and the occasional moan, nothing seemed too out of the ordinary.

"MacDonalds," she whispered. "In the other room."

Rage filled Ewan instantly. "How many?"

"Six perhaps. They came to whet their whistles, dip their wicks."

"And?" Ewan raised a brow.

"They've been talking a lot of nonsense, but enough to scare me and my lassies." She looked back at him, fear in her eyes. "Ye need to go. And ye need to go to Castle Gealach."

It was only then she seemed to notice what he was wearing.

"It's worse than I thought," she murmured.

Ewan didn't ask, because he had no doubt with the number of people Hildie saw in a given month, he was probably not the only one dressed oddly.

"Have ye got any spare clothes? 'Haps enough for two men, and maybe even a couple gowns?"

Hildie put her hands on her hips, her eyes lowering to slits as she tried to figure him out. "Getting greedy are ye?"

"Ye know I'm good for it. I'll bring ye the coin, double the coin. And I need provisions. A couple horses if ye have them."

Hildie stared at him hard, nothing getting passed her. "Who do ye have outside? Is it your wife? Ye need to get her to safety. The MacDonalds want her."

"More than her."

"Dear lord." Hildie crossed herself, a motion he'd never seen her do and never in all his days would have guessed she would. "Ye're going to owe me. If they find out I helped ye, they'll skin me alive and rape my dead body."

"I will give ye whatever ye want."

"No ye willna, because what I want, is tucked inside that awful getup ye're wearing." She pointed at his cock.

Ewan grinned. The same old Hildie. "Would ye settle for coin? I'd have to bring it back to ye from Gealach."

She nodded and winked. "A lot of it."

Hope surged. "Then ye'll help us?"

She jerked her head in a semblance of nod. "Ye're my favorite, always have been. Besides, I hate the MacDonalds with a passion. Wish every one of them would burn in a fiery, painful death. Come on." She grabbed his hand and led him to the back of the room toward a servant's entrance.

They walked through a storage room with several accesses, taking the door on the far left. It opened to the outside.

"Ye know where the stable is. If some of the horses go missing, what do I know about it? I'll gather some things over the next quarter hour and put them outside this door. I'll hold up a finger to let ye know how many more bags I've need to put out. When I make a zero, ye'll be coming to get the stock." Hildie continued to check her surroundings as she spoke and Ewan had the distinct impression this was not the first time she'd had to help someone escape. "I've got to make certain I'm not missed by the men in the other room, and I'll have my lassies keep them plenty busy. Lay low in the woods. Good luck. I dinna want to hear about your head on a spike. Nor that of the lass that claimed your heart. Ye're a good man, Ewan. If I was the type of woman who could love, I would have loved ye well."

Ewan grinned, leaned forward and kissed her cheek. "Ye did love me well, Hildie. I thank ye."

Hildie's eyes, for the briefest of moments, sparkled with unshed tears. "Go, ye sorry arse, afore I change my mind and force ye to give me the payment I truly want."

Ewan kissed her cheek once more, mumbled his thanks and then sprinted toward the woods. He cut his way back toward where he'd left his party, finding a rusty sword at his throat the moment they came into view.

"Good to see ye're on your game," he said to Rory, a tense smile on his face. "Try not to slice my head from my shoulders."

Rory quickly took the blade away. "Apologies. Heard someone sneaking up on us."

"We need to move quickly. The tavern is full of MacDonalds. Lucky for us, it's only a couple months past when we left."

"Thank god," Shona murmured.

"Nay. 'Tis not good at all. But let's get around the back first. We have to stay quiet."

The four of them stuck to the edge of the woods, just beyond the trees and out of sight, until they were close to the back of the tavern. Hildie opened the door and dropped a satchel. She held up two fingers, looking towards the woods but not seeing them, then shut the door.

"She'll be dropping more," Ewan whispered.

"Is that Hildie?" Shona asked.

"Aye. Since we've been gone, Logan declared war on the MacDonalds. He thinks we were taken by them, and the MacDonalds are plenty happy to wage war, but they want something else."

"What?" Rory asked.

"They're looking for Shona."

"Me?"

"Aye, love."

"Why would they possibly want me?"

"There wasn't enough time to ask, and I'm not certain she was privy to it. They cannot know of your relation to the Bruce, so it must be your healing powers they seek. Or maybe any information ye hold on Rory." Though he spoke the words with confidence, Ewan was not at all confident in what he said. MacDonald had been able to ferret out the secrets of Gealach before, what's to say he didn't know about more of the country's deeply hidden secrets?

"Well, if I am one of those princesses, I'd be long dead," Shona said.

"Aye." Ewan didn't want to point out that they were not the only time-travelers. Nor did he want to point out that if she weren't one of those princesses, she and Moira could still be descendants, which would put them in line for the throne.

"He'll not be getting his hands on ye, love," Ewan said. "Ye needn't worry over it."

The back door opened and Hildie dropped another satchel, holding up one finger, then she disappeared.

"Why is she willing to help if the enemy is within her building?" Rory asked. "Are ye certain she's not buying them time to come and find us?"

Ewan shook his head. "She hates the MacDonalds. They rarely pay their bar tabs and stiff her lassies all the time, leave many of them with bruises which puts them off the bargaining table for the next customer."

"Makes sense then."

Shona looked at Ewan with raised brows, waiting for him to expand his answer, but Ewan just shrugged, and flashed her a rueful smile.

The back door opened once more, except this time, it wasn't Hildie but a MacDonald warrior—Ewan recognized the colors of his plaid, and a wicked scar from his temple right down and across his face to his jaw on the opposite side. He tripped over the two satchels, though managed to catch himself before he fell to the ground. The bloody bastard kicked the bags aside, and then whipped up his plaid to piss.

Shona and Moira both quickly hid their eyes.

Then the back door opened once more, and Ewan's breath stopped, his heart pounding. Hildie, immediately seeing the warrior, smiled at him with wicked intent and tried to beckon him back inside. But the man didn't want to be coddled. He grabbed the madam by her arm and yanked her all the way out the door, spinning her around and pressing her chest and face to the wall.

Moira gasped, hands covering her mouth, but Shona's reaction was quite different. Her face flamed red with rage, and she frowned so fiercely he thought she might demand he hand over his stolen sword so she could slay the bastard.

The MacDonald roughly slapped Hildie's behind, yanked her gown up, exposing her arse. He lifted his plaid, and even from here, they could see the drive of his hips as he entered her. A second later, his grunts could be heard across the clearing.

Ewan gritted his teeth. This was not what Hildie and her tavern were about. This was not paying for services. Though she'd beckoned the warrior inside, perhaps with the intent to seduce, Ewan was going to call this a bloody rape. And he wasn't going to stand for it.

"I'll be right back," he whispered.

Shona nodded, not trying to stop him. They'd witnessed enough horror themselves over the last year, and she'd had to protect herself plenty in the years she was alone.

Ewan was quiet as ran, hunched over, across the glen, a rusty dagger from one of the outlaws held in his grip. He didn't try to gain the man's attention, or fight him. He simply came up behind him and slit his throat.

"Are ye all right?" he said to Hildie as the man dropped.

She turned around, tears glistening in her eyes. "Nothing that I've not dealt with before."

"Ye dinna deserve that."

"I dinna deserve ye." She swiped at her nose and changed the subject. "I've got the last of your baggage here."

He wanted to offer her more, to tell her to come with him, but he knew she wouldn't leave her lassies, or her tavern. This place was her life.

"Ye've sacrificed so much for us today. I'll never be able to repay ye. All the coin in the world wouldna."

She smiled. "I'd have done it for free. Now, get your arses moving. I'll get rid of this bloke."

"Want me to bury him?"

"Nay, love. If the men in there are wanting to eat meat all day, now I've got a fresh killed boar to serve."

Ewan's stomach turned, but it was no less than the bloody MacDonalds deserved.

Hildie swiped the rest of her tears. Took a deep breath and then smiled winningly. "Take care of yourself, Ewan. I counted. There are at least six horses in the stable. Might need to take 'em all if ye catch my meaning."

"Whatever ye ask."

"These bastards aren't going anywhere for awhile. We've been dousing their ale with poppies, but I guess we need to up the ante."

"Smart choice."

"Go on now. Go."

Ewan grabbed hold of the satchels and hurried back to the woods, when he turned around, Hildie was pointing out the dead body to a large, round man—James, Ewan thought his name might be. The cook.

"What is she going to do with the body?" Rory asked.

"Serve him to his friends with a fine wine sauce."

## ❧ 12 ❧

### SHONA

"**C**an we not do anything for her?" Shona asked, imploring Ewan. "At least let me give her a tincture that will ensure—"

"The bastard did not have time to finish," her husband said, understanding her meaning that she'd not want Hildie to suffer from having the MacDonald's child. "Besides, love, she most likely has a tincture of her own against such things."

Of course Shona's mind then went to disease, but how could she help Hildie against that now? In her profession, she was bound to come across any number of compromised men. And that got Shona's gears going. Once they were safe, and they understand the reason why they'd all been brought together, then she would come back here with an immunity tea for all the women, to help boost their immune systems and even perhaps, she could figure out a way to make pseudo-penicillin. If the Scottish scientist who'd discovered it had found it by using a certain type of mold—molds in England where he'd worked were probably the same right?—certainly Shona could, too.

"We're not safe here." Moira was the one who spoke now,

her face as pale as a wind-whipped linen sheet. She kept peering back toward the tavern, jumping at the slightest change in the wind.

Rory took her hand, and Shona observed the way her sister's knuckles turned white from gripping onto him so tightly. She was glad they'd found each other again. Shona had never seen her sister so happy as when she was with Rory.

"I'll go with Ewan to get the horses," he whispered to Moira. "Then we can leave."

She nodded, though she didn't let go.

The men picked up the satchels and, keeping their senses alert, led Shona and Moira back to the woods. Ewan had always been overprotective of her, even when she'd showed her skill time and again. She thought it was adorable.

"Stay hidden," Ewan said, pulling her into his embrace so she could breathe in the scent of his skin.

"I will."

"Your sister needs ye, lass. She's still in shock, I think."

Shona agreed. "It will take some time."

"Almost be better if she arrived the way ye and I did."

"In some ways, maybe. But perhaps this is a clue we were meant to return here. Or do ye think it means we're all meant to get back to modern day?"

"All of us?"

Shona shrugged. "Would ye want to?"

Ewan's jaw muscle flexed. "I dinna know." He kissed her quickly on the mouth and thrust the dagger from the outlaws into her hands. "Kill anyone who approaches ye."

Shona nodded, avoiding looking at Moira and Rory's exchange. The men hurried off, leaving the two of them alone in the silence of the woods, a view of the tavern through the branches.

"Are ye all right?" she asked her sister.

Moira blew out a breath that could have been a gale wind. "Getting there."

"I know this is sudden and it doesn't make sense, but, look at me." Moira raised her eyes from where they rested on her clenched fingers. "I'm all right, and ye will be, too."

"I want to go home," Moira said.

"What is home?"

Moira pressed her lips together, not answering the question. "Mrs. MacArthur has likely spread all sorts of rumors about us now."

"The meddling biddy is having the time of her life, I'm certain. She loves to be in everyone's business."

"This is true."

Suddenly, the hair on the back of Shona's neck was standing on end. "Shh." She quietly motioned to her sister, and then turned in a circle scanning their surroundings.

The tree leaves rustled, a few birds chirped. Laughter sounded in the distance, which was a good sign that the men at the tavern were not yet missing their friend. Still, something didn't feel right.

Ewan and Rory wouldn't have returned so quickly already.

She waved for her sister to come behind her, and without having to explain, Moira put her back to Shona's as they slowly turned in a circle. Foe in the woods did not always mean man, or woman. It could be a boar, a bear, sometimes a wildcat, if one were high up in the mountains. They stilled, listening for anything that might sound out of the norm.

And then she heard it. The subtle lift and settle of footsteps upon the forest floor. Human footsteps. They were being stalked. Anyone walking normally, would not try to use lichen and patches of grass to soften their footfalls. They should have talked quieter!

Shona swallowed hard, the dagger gripped tight in her fist. She was not going to allow her sister to be harmed.

"I have Rory's *sgian dubh*," Moira whispered so softly it could have been a shift in the wind.

Shona nodded, then reached back and squeezed her sister's hand, a subtle inference that she understood. They were going to take down whoever it was.

Swallowing aside her fear and breathing in a fresh breath of courage, Shona called out, "We can hear ye. Ye might as well make yourself known."

Cool laughter sounded somewhere off to her right. She shifted in that direction, not wanting her sister to be the one to face the foe head-on when Shona had so recently been involved with learning to survive in this era.

"Who left two lassies alone in the woods? Is this a new treat Hildie's offering?" The man made no attempt to hide his steps now, and soon he appeared before them. A scraggly beard that looked in need of a serious trim—and perhaps trapped a vermin or two—long ragged hair in much the same shape, a pimply-looking nose and eyes as swampy as a bog. He wore a filthy linen shirt and a plaid that had seen better days. His sword swung at his hips and the scent coming off him was an equal combination of filth and ale.

As Shona figured it, she and Moira had three choices: run; fight; or pretend they were Hildie's whores to distract the man until they took him down.

Judging by his appearance and scent, she decided to go with all three. He should be pretty easy to chop down. And at the very least, they could stall. "Well, why do ye think she's dressed us in breeches? It's a new treat for ye called, Catch the *Sassenach*."

"Och, I like the sound of that." His grin was hungry and desperate, oozing of villainous intent.

On instinct, Shona knew if this man got ahold of them, he would be certain to make the pain last.

She worked hard not to shudder, and surprisingly Moira did not tremble against her back.

"Close your eyes, and count to twenty. Then ye can open them and come after us." Shona winked for good measure.

The burly brute stared at her a moment, assessing all of her parts while licking his lips. "What if I dinna want to play the catch part, just get to the fucking?"

"I'm afraid that's against the rules," Shona said.

The man's face flattened and his cold, fathomless eyes met hers, his voice taking a chill note. "There are no rules out here, bitch."

And that was when she realized they should run.

"Moira," she ground out, and then the two of them were running, crashing through the forest in the direction their men had gone, the ogre trampling the forest floor behind them.

He was fast. Much faster than she would have guessed he'd be.

"Faster," Moira said, inching ahead.

"I'm right behind ye," Shona called.

But she was lying. Shona stopped short, whirled around and presented the bastard with her dagger. He skidded to a stop, hands out to protect himself from her blade.

"Take another step and I'll gut ye," she said through bared teeth.

A slow grin creased his brutal face. "Ye'll do as ye're told, ye filthy whore."

Though inside she was shaking, Shona held her ground. She'd faced off with men more fierce than this maggot before. "I dinna take kindly to ye talking to me that way."

"I dinna care." He loomed forward, and Shona didn't hesitate.

She lashed out, wielding the knife as she'd learned to do over the years, and slicing into the man's palms. He yelped, leaping backward, but only for a moment before he was on her again, fists wailing, and she was ducking out of the way. His arrogance at not even reaching for his own weapon fueled her fury. The whoreson truly thought he could take her down with his bare hands, even after she'd wounded him.

Remembering what Rory had taught her, what Ewan had expanded on, she dodged his blows, even dropping down and swiping at his shins with her blade, seeing the ribbons of red break free. As she ducked and dodged, Moira suddenly leapt from nowhere, a massive log in her hands. She brought the wood down on the bastard's head in a thunderous crack.

The oaf stood for a moment, transfixed, his eyes watering as he stared at them both, and then like a mighty oak that's been cut at its base, he fell forward with a loud thump to the ground.

"Thank ye," Shona said, breathless. She stooped to wipe the blood staining her blade on the grass.

"When did ye learn to fight so skillfully?" Moira asked, shock in her expression. "Ye were always wily, but I've never seen ye move like that."

"Here. With Rory." Shona frowned. "It's a harsh world, Moira. Not easy. But, to be honest, it's one I've come to love. And the people, I care about them. I've forged a life here."

"What about your life back home?" Moira nudged the brute with her booted foot.

He didn't so much as budge.

"This is my home now."

The look of sharp sadness that filled Moira's features was one she'd never wanted to see, nor be the cause of.

"I don't expect ye to understand," Shona said, rising to stand.

"I know ye don't. But I think I do." Moira dropped the wood. "Understand, I mean."

"Really?"

Moira's expression was thoughtful. "Home is where ye make it. Right? Home is with your people."

"That is true. But ye're one of my people. My constant companion, my very best friend."

Moira smiled sadly. "And now that position falls to your husband."

"Aye, he is my companion and best friend, too. But he could never replace the bond we have. That's different. We shared a womb. We shared a life."

"I don't think I can stay here," Moira's voice cracked. "I'm sorry."

Shona shook her head, reaching for her sister, and stepping over the downed arsehole in order to get to her. They clung to each other, tears of gratitude, relief, and fear, causing a maelstrom of sobs between the two of them.

"Ye dinna have to be sorry for wanting to go back to the place ye call home."

"But I am!" Moira sobbed. "I might never see ye again!"

Shona didn't have the heart to tell her sister that she'd been here in this time for six years before Fate felt the need to call her back, and for less than twenty-four hours at that. There was no telling when Moira would return to present day, if she'd stay here, or be whisked back another hundred years. Neither of them had the answers, and right now, all Shona could be grateful for was the fact that her sister *did* finally believe her. Now they could really begin the healing process before figuring out where the hell they were supposed to be in history's timeline.

"What's happened?" Ewan burst through the trees, his tone urgent, followed by Rory's, "Bloody hell!"

Shona wiped at her tears, smiling at her sister, before reassuring Ewan. "We're fine, I promise. He didn't hurt us."

"We didn't give him the chance." Moira nodded to the thick log beside the ogre's head.

"I'm impressed." Rory nudged the man with his foot.

Ewan grabbed Shona's shoulders. "Are ye certain ye're all right?"

"Positive."

But that didn't stop him from looking her body over, checking for wounds.

"Enough," she said with a laugh, brushing his exploring hands aside. "Did ye get the horses?"

"Aye, but we left them tied a few dozen yards away. We came running as soon as we heard the struggle." Ewan kissed her softly. "I was scared to death."

"I admit to a small amount of fear myself." She bobbed her head toward the man. "But ye and Rory both taught me well. And I have Moira to thank for the blow that finally knocked him out."

Ewan chuckled and kissed her again. "All in one piece."

"Aye."

"I hate to interrupt," Rory said. "But if we dinna ride soon, we'll not make it to Castle Gealach before dark."

"I dinna want my wife on the road after dark," Ewan said. Then he swung her up into his arms and started walking toward where they'd hidden the horses.

"Put me down! I'm perfectly capable of walking."

He winked at her. "I know ye are. I just like to hold ye, especially after a scare like that."

Shona snuggled against her husband and peered over his shoulder, watching the way Moira smiled softly, glancing at the ground and then at Rory from the sides of her eyes, almost shy. Rory was doing the same sort of thing in his own way—holding his breath after speaking, waiting for her answer, blowing it out when she finally did. They were acting as though they didn't know each other. Which was funny, because the two of them had been hot and heavy before Rory left. Shona could see in their exchanges that they still loved each other. If only the two of them could say it. Or maybe they didn't quite realize it yet.

Perhaps a little more time, which she wasn't certain they had, would be all it took to push them back together.

"I love ye, Ewan," she whispered against her husband's ear and then laid her head on his shoulder.

"I love ye, too."

For Shona, it didn't matter where she was, as long as Ewan was by her side.

## 13

## RORY

The sun was just beginning its descent to the horizon when they crested the ridge overlooking the castle below. Rory breathed out a sigh of relief that they'd made it back to the castle with all of the MacDonald horses, and not a single incident to waylay them.

While they'd stopped to water the horses some miles back, they'd all changed into the clothing Hildie had supplied them. The plaids were Grant colors, not surprising, and clean. The ladies ended up with gowns that were rather more innocent than Rory would have thought possible coming from a tavern full of willing wenches.

"Wow." Moira gasped with pleasure.

Rory glanced at Moira, wanting to take in the exact expression of awe on her face.

"I've seen this place, but it's so different. So incredibly majestic. I can't believe it! I've only ever seen it with walls crumbling, no roof..." Wonderment brightened her features.

"Aye. Isn't it amazing what five hundred years can do to a place?" Rory chuckled and jutted his chin toward the castle. "I remember the first time I journeyed to your time, I could have been whisked off of Earth, taken to the moon for all I knew."

"Ye jest," Moira said, "but they are already talking about setting up bases on the moon and other planets."

"Other planets?" Rory raised a brow, his gaze setting on the sky above, imagining a sky full of places like this. "Are they like ours?"

"There are thousands, maybe millions of other planets in all the galaxies. But so far they've not found any exactly like ours. Maybe a couple close to it. Who knows what they'll find. If time travel is possible, why not other planets?"

"Lass, ye've just blown my mind."

Moira laughed, and so did Ewan and Shona. In the group of four, Rory was the only one originally from the 1500's. What did that say about their group? What could it mean? Though their customs, cultures, entire ways of life were infinitely different in the various time periods, that didn't matter, because at the root of it all, people were people.

Rory turned his attention back to Gealach, the spires on the gates sparkling. "One of these days, I will pick your brain more about that."

"If I'm still here." Moira said it so casually, as though she were saying that it may rain tomorrow, but the words themselves, they cut deep.

Rory grunted, unable to form a true response. *If she was still here.* He didn't want to think about a world without her in it. He wanted her with him always. Somehow, he had to make her see that they were meant to be together. This was Fate's act, now he had to prove it. But ultimately, she had to make that decision herself—he didn't want her any other way but willing.

He urged his horse forward, following Ewan and Shona who would speak to the Master of the Gate.

"Remember, dinna say ye are Rory MacLeod to anyone,

save the laird," Ewan said. "If Logan is at home, I'll request a meeting and see what we can get sorted. Logan can offer ye protection while ye're here."

Rory would be lying if he didn't admit that the offer of protection from a laird stung two ways. One, he didn't want to cower behind the boots of another man, and two, the last laird he'd sworn to protect had ended up dead. If Logan Grant offered him protection, in turn, Rory would kneel before him and pledge his own loyalty and protection, an oath he wasn't certain he could commit to, given his past.

He cleared his throat, and offered his thanks anyway.

They reached the front of the gate, the portcullis closed tight, with the dimming light of gloaming giving their surroundings a dusky gray aura.

"Who goes there?" shouted the man at the top of the gate.

Ewan raised his arm. "Taig! 'Tis Ewan."

There was silence for a breath, and then the man leaned over the ramparts staring down, a mischievous grin on his face. "Ewan? Ewan who?"

"Ewan Fraser, ye jackanapes!"

"My wife must have poisoned my whisky, for surely I'm dead!" the man shouted down. "Ye've been gone for months! Thought the MacDonald had fed ye to his pack of demons."

"'Tis I, in the flesh. I assure ye, ye're not dead, though I canna tell ye if your wife is poisoning ye. If I were the lass, I'd have done it long ago."

Taig laughed. "It is ye, captain! Open the gates!"

The portcullis was raised, the gates opened, and before they could cross under, a rush of men-at-arms crowded through the opening, surrounding them.

They lifted Ewan from his horse, and Shona, too, chanting and carrying them through the throng. Rory nodded to the men who took his and Moira's reins. She looked at him fearfully and he smiled, winked, hoping it would be reassuring enough.

"Where the hell have ye been?" Taig asked Ewan.

"Bloody *Sassenachs*," Ewan answered, the menace in his voice so convincing Rory almost believed it, too.

"And your friends?"

"Moira is Shona's sister, twins can ye not tell?"

"Aye, the spitting image, save for the hair. And the man?"

"I'm—" Rory started, but was cut off by Shona.

"My sister's husband."

Nobody asked his name, and when Rory thought he might have panicked at being so quickly married, he did not. In fact, the idea of being Moira's husband sat very well with him. He flicked his gaze toward Moira to gauge her reaction. Stock still, her expression was blank. Rory felt conflicting feelings of being both impressed at her ability to hide any shock she might be feeling, and sadness that the thought of being married to him hadn't brought a smile to her face. Well, what could he expect?

"Come inside, we'll get ye something to eat."

"Ewan! Shona!" A woman, dressed in a fine gown, her hair swept up in a knot of fiery curls upon her head, rushed down the wide stone stairs of the keep. "I can't believe it's you!"

A *Sassenach*? Rory had not known the mistress of Gealach, married to the Guardian of Scotland, was English.

A formidable warrior stepped from inside the castle onto the landing, staring down the stairs at them, his expression unreadable, his stance rigid.

"We've searched all of Scotland for ye. They said ye were abducted. Simply vanished." Logan's expression was guarded, his mouth set in a firm line.

There was a brief exchange of glances between Emma and Shona, a clear question and answer.

Emma was a time-traveler. She must have guessed that was what happened.

Rory was a little worried about how they'd be received by Logan Grant. He didn't appear as pleased as Ewan had led Rory to believe he would be.

The Lady of Gealach broke the tension. "And ye've brought guests," Emma said wrapping her arms around Shona's shoulders.

"Please allow them to stay, my lady," Shona murmured. "My sister and her husband."

Moira kept her gaze shifting from the ground to Shona's face and back again. Nervous, her hands were tightly clutched in front of her hips. Rory wanted to pick her up and whisk her away from all this, back to a world where she didn't have to be scared, or worried. A world where he could protect her more easily. Then again, her world had its dangers, too.

Emma graced them all with an enchanting smile. "Of course they can stay."

"Maybe they canna," Logan said from the top of the stairs. "Ewan. Glad ye've returned. A word? And with your new friend."

Not a good sign. Rory's gut twisted.

"Aye, my laird." Ewan jerked his head at Rory.

Rory followed behind, eager to get his conversation with the Guardian finished. The inside of the castle was dark and gloomy; a contrast to their lady's welcome, though he did smell fresh flowers and rushes. Logan led them up a circular stone stair and down another dimly lit corridor corridor to a room he opened with a key. Once inside, Logan walked to a sideboard and poured whisky in three metal cups, but before he offered them, he downed his own and then refilled.

"What happened, Ewan? Emma was worried for ye. We all were. I had our armies searching the entire damned country.

Accused MacDonald of taking ye. Even got the regent involved. He'll be cross to know I falsely accused the man."

"If I could have stopped the chain of events, my laird, I would have. Ye know that. I hope ye can find it possible to forgive me, to pardon my wife and her family." Ewan came forward, smacked Logan on the back and said jovially, obviously trying to lighten the mood, "Did ye miss me?"

Logan glowered a full five seconds. "Dammit, I thought the MacDonalds had gotten hold of ye." The two men quickly embraced amid much backslapping, and then Logan gave them each their cups. "Who are ye?" he demanded of Rory.

Rory stood straighter. "I'm Rory MacLeod."

The shift in the laird's demeanor was not subtle. A storm filled his face. "Ewan. Explain."

"I'd rather do so myself, my laird," Rory said, bracing for the backlash of having spoken when not addressed.

Logan grunted, but there was no other response, and Rory took that as an affirmative to keep going.

"I've not heard the rumors about myself, other than what Ewan has told me. I am no murderer. But I have betrayed my clan."

Logan said nothing, simply glowered in Rory's direction. The cup in Rory's hand remained there, though he desperately would have preferred a deep sip to take the edge off. Aye, the man was about his own size, and their skills could have been matched for all he knew, but to take on the Guardian of Scotland would be paramount to naming himself a traitor to his country, and that he certainly was not.

"Like Ewan, I was captain of the guard. There was a siege at our castle. The enemy broke through our defenses; they began to ravage the village. Tear the castle apart. The children were hurried into hiding, but my laird, and his mistress, they stood strong. They were taken when I was in the midst of combat." Rory's mouth had gone dry. "I called to the men left standing to come with me to get our laird and his wife back. But that left our people defenseless, and when the enemy saw us pursuing, they cut down my laird, and his wife. They fought us, left us for dead. It was carnage. When I woke, I was badly wounded. I tried to make it back, but... I couldn't. By the time I was well enough, it was too late. So much time had passed. I... I ran. I couldn't bear it. I was the cause of so much destruction."

"Ye were not the cause." Logan sipped his whisky. "Drink."

"'Tis kind of ye to say such, but I was. If I'd—"

"Stop. Too many times we say, *if only*. There is no going back, only forward. I dinna believe the accusations of murder against ye. I've a skill for judging, and I can see ye're innocent. Ye were going after your laird, his wife—to save them, not to harm them. Your sworn duty is to protect them, anyone should understand that. But, ye see, MacLeod's son, Ranulf, the new laird, does not believe it. What reason would he have to consider that ye killed the MacLeod and his wife?"

This was a part of Rory's life that was best left in the dark hole he'd buried it in. Rory raised his chin, not speaking.

"I canna help ye if ye dinna tell me everything." Logan Grant was a formidable man and the way he spoke so calmly, and still managed to lace a bit of a threat into his words spoke volumes.

If Rory were less of a man, he might have been frightened. But he wasn't.

Rory had heard many stories about Logan. About his domination on the fields of battle, how he'd risen to the top, even rumors that he was the rightful king. But all of those factors did not make Rory want to divulge his secrets.

"I'll take my chances," Rory said, straightening to his full height. "I appreciate your offer of help—"

"Dinna be a fool!" Ewan seethed. "Ye canna survive. There is a price on your head. Ranulf MacLeod will take ye dead or alive."

Rory gritted his teeth. "I'm not a man to cower behind the power of another. I will fight this on my own."

"Think of Moira," Ewan continued. "What about her?"

"She is not your concern." Rory fisted his hands, not liking the direction this conversation was taking.

Logan's cool voice cut through the heat of Rory's anger. "She will be if ye go off and get yourself killed."

Give up his pride, or the woman he loved?

That was not a choice Rory wanted to make.

"She'd be safer without me." The words were out of his mouth before the thought had fully formed. "I loved her once, I love her still, but perhaps 'tis best for us to part ways. She'll be free to return to her... home."

Ewan shook his head.

Logan sipped his whisky, thoughtful.

Rory downed his drink in one swill, not daring to ask for a refill, though Logan poured him one anyway.

"I had the same thoughts once," Logan said. "Why bring danger to the ones we love? They're safer outside of the realm of danger. But the truth is, they are not. Because we love them, they are in more danger. Your wife will be the victim of MacLeod, just as Shona could have been."

Ewan jerked his gaze from Rory to Logan.

Logan continued. "Anyone with an association to ye is already compromised. Being that the four of ye are now under my roof, that means that the entirety of my clan is now at more risk of war from MacLeod, at the verra least a visit, which he's been itching to do since I accused him anyhow. Your arrival is tantamount to an invitation."

"I will leave at once." Rory set down his cup on the sideboard and marched toward the door.

"Stop." Logan's voice had taken a turn for harsh. "I'll lock ye in my dungeon if I have to. But we both know the easiest way to solve this dilemma is for ye to simply tell me why the young laird would think ye killed his parents. Then, I can help ye."

Rory had stopped walking, but he couldn't turn around. He stared hard at the door, needing more than anything to be on the other side of it.

"Come on, man," Ewan said.

"What ye say will not leave the room," Logan added. "Ye have my word."

Rory swallowed hard around the barbs that seemed to have implanted in his throat. He'd never told anyone before, and he didn't want to tell anyone now. A secret that should have been locked away, that was buried alongside the bodies of the laird and mistress of MacLeod.

Moira's face flashed into his mind. Her smile. Her hesitant touch to his hand. She was slowly starting to trust him. He couldn't put her in danger, even if it meant that she might find out the truth and choose never to be with him again.

"The laird wants me dead," he admitted.

Logan crossed his arms over his chest. "Aye, we gathered that."

"Because I..."

They waited patiently as Rory searched for the words. "Because I am his father, which means his right to be laird of the MacLeod clan could be questioned." His throat burned from the admission.

"Ye're his father?" Logan's voice was steady, not even a hint of shock.

"Aye."

"How?" Ewan asked, his surprise not as well hidden as his laird's.

"When I was a lad, the laird, my uncle, took me under his

wing. He'd just married a young lass about my age, I was four-teen or fifteen summers at the time. She was beautiful, and we ended up spending a lot of time together." Rory paused, wishing he'd not gotten rid of his whisky cup.

"That does not make him your son."

"Aye, but it does. Ye see, when she conceived, her husband was on campaign. We made love everyday for the two months that he was gone."

"Ah. Did the old laird know?" Logan questioned, while Ewan remained silent, contemplative.

This was the hardest part. "Aye. He did. And he accepted it. He embraced the lad as his own, after all there is a blood connection, and he continued to promote me within the clan."

"Did they have any other children?"

Rory shook his head. "Nay. In fact, one drunken night, the laird confessed to me he did not think he could have children, and that was why he paired me with his lady wife. He was hoping it would happen so he'd have a son to claim his place, and if there was a blood tie, all the better."

"Why would he not simply name ye as laird?"

"He'd been married before, and they did not conceive, and I'd been his only heir, though I made it clear, in my hotheaded youth, I did not want the honor. I suppose he thought he was doing me a favor."

"Would ye have accepted the position if the clan asked?"

Rory shrugged. "I'd not thought about it. 'Twas always the plan for Ranulf as heir."

"Does Ranulf know?"

"Aye. His father confessed on his deathbed, and swore to Ranulf that no one knew."

"Then why should the young laird want ye dead?"

"Because I am still a threat, and because he believes I dishonored his mother. If the truth were to come out his position would be in jeopardy, not to mention his mother's reputation. We do not speak ill of the dead. He looks the spitting image of myself. Perhaps 'tis shame. And every time he looks at his own reflection, he is reminded that I am still alive. To erase the shame, he must kill me." Rory shrugged. "It does not matter to him that his position is one I'd never take."

"Why not? It is rightfully yours."

"If I could not save my uncle, why should I take his place? 'Tis part of the reason I've never gone back. Perhaps I carry a bit of shame myself."

"I am not going to question your reasons for making the choice ye did, but your uncle's death does not mean ye'd have been a poor laird," Logan said.

Ewan handed him another large dram of whisky. "Thank ye for trusting us with your secret."

Rory locked eyes with Logan. "If something should happen to me, swear to keep Moira safe."

"She will always have my protection."

"Ye have my gratitude." Rory bent to one knee placing his hand over his heart. "And my loyalty. I pledge ye my allegiance and my life."

"Stand." Logan reached out and Rory clasped his forearm. "I would not have required your pledge to keep her safe."

"All the same, I am obligated to give it."

"As one of us, I will help ye to clear your name," Logan swore.

Rory nodded and shot the rest of his whisky down his throat. Facing his past, a son who wanted him dead, telling Moira the truth, that was going to require a lot more than a few shots of whisky.

## 🦋 14 🦋

### MOIRA

"**Y**ou traveled again didn't you?" Lady Emma asked after clearing her solar of servants.

Moira and Shona stood before the window, glasses of wine in their hands. Moira was still in a state of awe. The castle was mesmerizing, the furniture ornate, the views spectacular, and Emma, she looked as though she belonged here in her green woolen long skirts with the Grant plaid embroidered at her cuffs. Her teeth were clean, quite unlike what Moira had thought of women in history, though since she'd time traveled, she'd likely brought her hygiene habits with her.

Moira looked down at her own gown, a ruddy red, with dark, brown leather lacings over the front, and a looped leather belt that matched. Moira thought it was like playing dress up when she was young, only she got to drink wine—which tasted so much different than what she bought at the liquor store back home. It was fresher, more vibrant. She took another sip, savoring the flavor on her tongue. French wine be damned, she'd take a 1544 Scottish merlot. That thought made her giggle.

But the somber gazes of Emma and Shona pulled her back to the conversation, and she stopped all at once.

"Yes," Shona confessed. "Back to my time. It's where we found Moira and Rory. As soon as we were all together, it happened again, bringing us back here."

"Then this must be where you belong." Emma slid her hands over the skirts of her gown, the roundness of her pregnant belly very pronounced. "I've only traveled the once, and never gone back."

"And I've traveled here and back and here again," Shona said.

"I've only done this once," Moira offered, though she refused to believe this was where she belonged. Edinburgh and the twenty-first century beckoned.

There had to be a way to get back there. She wasn't sure when it happened, perhaps with the feeling of hunger, or needing to pee—and using a leaf Shona gave her to wipe—but she'd finally come to terms with what had happened. She'd time traveled. A miracle or a curse?

"We are all together now," Emma said, beaming a smile. "And Ewan... He..." She chewed her lip and then took a sip of her heavily watered down wine.

Moira glanced at Shona, what could Emma have wanted to say about Ewan? No one had told her that he was her brother yet? Shona shook her head, almost imperceptible in its slight motion. Wow. Someone should have told her. All this time he'd been right there with her.

Emma had lost so much in that plane crash—her parents and her brother, she deserved to know that he was still alive. But that wasn't Moira's call, or her right to reveal.

The lady of the castle cleared her throat delicately. "The men are talking, I'm certain, about where you've been. Did you all come up with a story?"

Moira nodded while Shona answered. "Captured by the English, we escaped."

"And how did you come across your sister."

Moira stared at the beautiful emerald ring on Emma's finger. It glittered in the candlelight, mesmerizing her.

"We'll say we passed by our old cottage and found her and Rory there, looking for us."

Emma pursed her lips. "That sounds believable."

"Aye."

Their mistress let out a whimsical sigh. "Tell me of modern day. What was it like? I miss it sometimes, though I wouldn't give up Logan for anything."

"Busy," Shona said with a slight smile. "Loud. I feel the same way. I'm not going anywhere if I can help it."

Moira hadn't thought of that difference. It was a lot quieter here. Like, *a lot,* more quiet, and yet, her thoughts were so much louder she'd hardly noticed. "Where are ye from, Emma?"

"The U.S."

"That is why they think you're a, what did they call it, a *Sassenach?*" Moira asked.

Emma nodded, setting her wineglass down and fiddling with her hair.

"Does Logan know?"

"Yes."

"So why don't we tell him the truth about me and Rory? About Ewan?" She flicked her gaze toward Shona whose eyes widened. Her sister needn't worry. Ewan's secret was his to tell.

"I think we should." Emma stood up and grabbed a handful of nuts from a bowl. "He did search all of Scotland for you. But he also searched the glens."

"Did he find anything?" Shona asked.

Emma nodded. "At the glen at the top of the ridge

beyond, with the sacred stone. He found your belongings. The men with him assumed the bastard MacDonalds had abducted you and stripped you of your belongings so no one would recognize you."

Shona helped herself to some of the nuts, and Moira admired the bowl. They did look fresh, but her stomach was so twisted in knots the thought of eating only made her queasy.

"I can see why they would think so," Shona said.

"What were you doing up there? Why didn't you tell anyone?" Emma's gaze didn't waver, the same intense stare Moira had seen from Ewan. They were definitely related.

Shona's face heated and Moira looked at her sister, keenly interested in what her answer would be. Why would she be embarrassed? And then it dawned on her and Moira gasped, the back of her hand to her lips.

"Do tell, Shona. I'd also like to know the answer to this, since ye showed up in Edinburgh naked."

Emma giggled. "Naked? Oh, what I wouldn't give to see that." She winced and pressed her hand to her belly. "Ouch. Energetic little baby."

"How far along are ye?" Moira asked.

"About eight months now."

"And no medical care." That was something Moira couldn't handle.

"The midwife here is a dream." Emma rolled her eyes.

Shona and Moira laughed.

"Thank God for your sister. I'd have warned Logan off me if she weren't here. But let us not get off track. Tell me what happened, you know, with the glen," Emma said.

"After ye told me about the powerful magic of the glen"— Shona pointed to Emma's round belly—"I wanted to see if it could help us in conceiving a child. We snuck out of the castle, not wanting to be disturbed."

"Ah," Emma said, sinking onto one of her chaise lounges. "So when ye traveled ye were in the middle of having sex."

Moira pressed her lips together to keep from laughing at the image that conjured. To have been there and seen the looks on the people's faces as her sister and her husband showed up mid-coitus in the park.

Shona rolled her eyes. "No, we'd already fallen asleep."

"Well, do you think it worked?" Emma asked.

Shona stared at Emma's belly, envy and joy filling her eyes. "I don't know. I won't know for a couple of weeks I guess."

"More like a few months without a pregnancy test." Emma stuffed a few more almonds into her mouth, chewing as she contemplated some thought. "I missed my period, but it wasn't the first time. I think with the stress of being here, I wasn't so regular. Anyways, it wasn't until it had been a few months missed and that I felt a little flutter in my belly that I was certain."

"What about morning sickness?" Moira asked.

"Well there was a little bit of that, but I couldn't be sure if it was just being ill or not. I had, and still do, a lot of heart-burn. Shona was making me up a concoction for that before she disappeared."

"Oh, I did make that for ye!"

Emma smiled. "I found it."

"Did it help?"

"Yes, very much. Thank you." Emma jumped up from her chaise, a little too quickly as she swayed on her feet. "Whoops. Keep forgetting how off balance I am."

Shona helped to steady Emma on her feet. "Well, let's go find the men, and we can see if they told Logan the truth."

As Emma approached the door, there came a swift knock. Upon opening the door, Logan, Ewan and Rory filed in.

"We were just coming to see you." Emma beamed at her

husband who touched her belly and bent to kiss her gently on the lips.

The sight made Moira smile. Amazing that a woman could find happiness living in the past. Moira had always believed one should go forward, live for the now, the present. Well, she supposed, even if they were living in the past, this *was* their present.

Her gaze fell on Rory. He was regarding her with a sentiment she didn't want to recognize but did all the same. Love. Appreciation. Admiration. He looked so handsome standing there. His muscles bulging from the too tight *leine* shirt he'd gotten from Hildie, the kilt a little too short. Moira let out the breath she'd been holding. Time didn't seem to matter where he was concerned. She was just as attracted to him now as she was the first time she'd ever met him.

"May I present to ye, my laird," Ewan said, "The Ayreshire lassies."

Logan looked stricken. "Ayreshire?"

"Aye."

Rory's entire body stiffened and Moira found herself gravitating toward him. Why did he seem on the defensive? They could trust Logan, couldn't they?

"Ayreshire?" Emma asked. "What is the significance?"

Logan blew out a breath. "Love, ye remember that song?" He sang a few verses in Gaelic. "One of red and one of black, born at Ayreshire and swept back, lost forever the princesses of time, the last of the king's most sacred line."

"Yes?" Emma raised her brows, studying Shona and Moira with a questioning gaze.

"That is about the Ayreshire lassies. Princesses that went missing a hundred years ago."

"Oh..." Emma blew out a long breath. "You're them."

Moira shook her head. "We're not. We grew up in Edinburgh. We've been there as long as I can remember."

"How far back do ye remember?" Ewan asked Shona.

"Until I was five or six maybe?"

"What do ye remember? A family?" Logan asked.

"We lived in the foster care system," Shona answered.

"What is that?" Logan glanced at Emma for an answer.

Emma explained. "Families or people who take in orphaned children."

"So ye had no family?" Logan asked.

"We had each other." Moira felt her spine straightening with pride. "We are each other's family."

"I meant no offense," Logan explained. "'Tis simply a question of whether or not..." He broke off, and glanced at his wife who nodded.

"They have traveled," she blurted out.

No one made a sound, nor appeared shocked. Logan ought to know the truth.

"Ye know then?" Ewan asked.

Logan rubbed the stubble of his cheeks. "Aye, Emma has told me about it."

"And ye believe?" Ewan watched Logan intently.

"How could I not?"

Rory stepped closer to Moira, his little finger brushing hers. "There is a chance, if the both of ye dinna remember, that ye were brought to another time before ye were old enough to know, for protection. 'Haps what happened to Shona could have happened to ye both back then. Ye were made to forget. The same thing happened to—"

But Ewan cut Rory off before he could say more, perhaps fearful that his secret would be revealed. "What do ye think?"

Moira literally felt the blood draining from her face. "We have a large trust fund."

"Aye?"

"A very large one."

"Do ye think that ye were brought to another realm for protection? The money left to take care of ye?"

Moira dragged in a ragged breath. "I don't know." She reached up, tugging at the necklace she'd always thought belonged to her mother. "We've never known the identities of our parents. We have no pictures. No letters."

"What is that?" Logan stepped closer, examining the charm. "My god. It's true."

Rory caught Moira's fearful gaze. "Ye're the firstborn."

"What?"

"The firstborn was given a pendant that belonged to her mother, a golden circle to represent the crown with a lion etched on top of it to show the joined houses of Scotland and England." Logan let the pendant drop back against her chest. "Your blood could have united the countries, but your mother feared for your life. Your father was a prisoner of the English King Edward III. If Edward had known King David had children, he would have seen ye killed to keep his crown."

"Then how...?"

"Perhaps your mother had found out about time travel. Or, entrusted your care to someone who did. They brought ye to the future, set up a fund to keep ye taken care of for all of your life, away from danger."

The news weighed heavy. Orphans for as long as they could remember. Moira had never had hopes of a reunion with her parents, but every little lass could dream. That dream was now thoroughly squashed. Her parents had lived hundreds of years before, and Fate only sent one where it wanted one to go.

"The good news is no one should ever guess that ye are they." Logan winked. "Shall we dine? I'm certain my wife is famished."

## ❧ 15 ❧

### MOIRA

The next few days were filled with much napping, drinking wine, and generally avoiding a revisit of the conversations that had taken place upon their arrival. At least for Moira. She spent the days with Shona planting in the herb garden that had been mostly ignored since her sister left—since no one knew just what to plant—and concocting various herbal remedies in Shona's workroom.

Whenever Rory tried to approach her, Moira quickly turned the other way—a cowardly act that made her feel terrible. But she just couldn't face him. How would he feel about her, knowing that she'd been a princess? Was still a princess? He'd yet to share with her the full secrets of his past. It just seemed the chasm between them could never be closed if neither of them was willing to face the truth of their pasts. At least now she knew for certain he'd never left her to have a relationship with her sister. He'd not left her because he wanted to. He plainly had no choice in the matter. That knowledge was a relief. A liberation from the torment she'd been feeling for years. And perhaps time was the healing balm for her heart.

Moira strolled through the bailey. She'd decided to take a visit to the stable to feed the horses a few extra carrots she'd snagged from the garden when Cook wasn't looking. This was also something she'd decided she liked doing in the last few days. At night, she stared out her window toward the top of the ridge, the one that Shona and Ewan had been making love on that sent them to the future. Whenever there was another full moon, she was going to go to the top of that mountain, and if she had to strip down to her bare skin, she would. She'd decided. She'd miss her sister a lot. She'd miss Rory, too. But this was not the life she wanted to live. She didn't belong here.

Coming to that decision had not been easy.

"Moira."

So deep in thought was she that she'd not heard Rory's approach. She glanced up at him, admiring his dark eyes, pools of memories in their depths. A face that always made her smile. He held onto her arm gently, sliding down to her hand, threading his fingers in hers. Perhaps he was afraid she'd run, and why shouldn't he be, for she had every other time he'd tried to talk to her. Or maybe he just wanted to touch her as much as she wanted to touch him.

But she'd also decided that she wasn't going to run from him anymore. Especially if, within a few weeks, she might not ever see him again.

"Can we... talk?" The word almost sounded foreign on his tongue, for it came out sounding thick and awkward.

There was a little trickle of sweat on his temple and the collar around his shirt. The men had obviously been training. Now that was something she'd not seen yet, but was certain she would have enjoyed watching.

"Sure."

He glanced from side to side. "In private?"

Moira chewed her lip, thinking the stable a very private place already.

"Please? Ye dinna have to worry about your reputation as everyone thinks we're married."

"Unhappily," she said. Rory had been sleeping with the men in the barracks instead of in the chamber they'd been given to share. That was sure to have some tongues wagging.

"What goes on between the two of us is none of their concern."

She'd always loved that about him. The confidence to be himself and not give a shit what anyone else thought. She wanted to be more like that. "All right."

He let go of her hand and offered her his elbow. She stared at it, wanting to touch him, to be the one that reached out, but knowing that as soon as she did all those potent feelings would come tunneling back inside her. Rory patiently waited for the storm of her indecision to pass. Well, she'd already been holding his hand. His arm wasn't much different. She took his elbow simply because he was such a decent and kind man—and because the contact felt good, left her warm.

The moment her fingertips touched his bicep, heat suffused her limbs. He was strong, incredibly firm, and yet he could be so gentle.

"Where are ye taking me?" she asked.

"A place I've discovered over the last couple of days."

He walked her around the rear of the castle, through the gardens and to the postern gate. Once outside, there was a set of slick stone stairs leading down to the shore of the loch. She held on tight as they walked, taking each damp step very carefully, until they reached a marshy bottom.

The scent of the loch wafted over them in a calming breeze. Along the loch ducks swam in groups and pairs, bobbing under the water every once in awhile in search of food.

"I've been walking the shores. 'Tis soothing," he said.

"Yes." They walked arm in arm. With her free hand, she trailed her fingers over the reeds waving gently in the breeze.

"Moira, I've been thinking."

Her stomach did a little flip.

"I..." He cleared his throat and her stomach dropped. "I still love ye, lass. I want ye to be mine in more than just pretense."

She stiffened, her belly doing a little flip at his admission. Staring off into the distance, she whispered, "Love is not everything, Rory. I'm not a possession."

"That is not what I meant." He sounded hurt, and she felt immediately guilty for shunning his love.

Moira sighed. "I know." And she did. Rory was not that type of man. He wanted her to be his, not because he wanted to own her, but because he wanted to protect her and cherish her. To love her in earnest. And didn't she want that? Didn't she want to return those same feelings and gestures? The answer was an easy and resounding: *yes*.

Moira stopped walking, turning to face Rory. He was easily a foot taller than her; she'd always admired his wonderful height. She loved that he towered over her, it made her feel safe and when he wrapped his arms all the way around her, she could cuddle up against him and feel like nothing bad would ever happen.

"I'm sorry, Rory." Tears burned her eyes. "I know ye didn't mean it like that." She swiped at her tears. "I'm just scared. I don't know what's going to happen. I opened my heart before and—"

He started to interrupt, but she pressed her fingers to his lips.

"Please let me finish. I know it wasn't your fault that ye were called back to your time, but I spent years blaming ye and hurting, and those feelings are still fresh. I don't even know if I'll be here in the morning. I want to go home. I *like* living in modern times. I like medicine and my cell phone."

Rory nodded, his face falling. "Love, if ye want to live in the present, I'm willing to give up everything here to be with ye."

"I could never ask that of ye." Her voice cracked with emotion.

His hands slid from her elbows to her shoulders and then he tugged her forward into his embrace. "But I want ye to know that I speak the truth. That I would. Everything."

Moira wrapped her arms around him, sinking into his hold, her ear pressed to the sound of his beating heart. She closed her eyes, breathing out a contented sigh.

"I thank ye, Rory, from the bottom of my heart, I really do."

"I love ye. I know my disappearing hurt ye, and that the pain will take some time to ebb, but I want ye to know that. I love ye still, with all my heart."

Moira pressed a kiss over his heart, breathing in his familiar masculine scent, wanting to tell him that she'd never stopped loving him, but unsure how to say it without crying or falling apart. She wasn't ready to make that kind of verbal commitment, and Rory didn't seem to be asking for one. She hoped that her small kiss showed just how much she actually felt, without having to say the words.

"Did ye hear that?" Suddenly Rory stiffened, his hand went to his sword and his eyes scanned the horizon.

Moira inched away from his chest to look and listen, not seeing or hearing what he did.

"What is it?"

"Horses. Maybe a dozen of them."

"Is that unusual?" What did she know, there seemed to be horses everywhere.

"It's hard to explain. Horses are not unusual, but we are not expecting anyone."

"Are ye certain?"

"Aye. I've been...working with Ewan and Logan."

Working? What did he mean by that? "Does this have to do with MacLeod?"

Rory met her gaze, his brow furrowed, eyes filled with concern. "Aye, lass."

"Should I be worried?"

"There is something I have to tell ye." He threaded a hand through his hair, blowing out a harsh breath.

Her heart skipped a beat. Whatever it was sounded as though it would be intense and she braced herself, trying to keep her cool. She placed her hands on his chest and said, "I will listen."

"My uncle was—"

A horn blew from the top of the castle.

"What was that?"

"They are arming the gates. We have to go." He looked so conflicted. "But ye must know..."

"Ye can tell me later. Rory, whatever it is, it won't change in the next moment."

But he didn't look so convinced. "It will have to wait. Your safety is top priority."

Rory grabbed her hand and they ran along the shore to the rocky stairs. Moira tried to keep pace with him, but for every stride of his, she had to take two. When she tripped on the fourth stair, he swept her up into his arms and ran the rest of the way up and then through the postern gate.

"Ye can put me down. Go. See what's happening. I'll be along shortly."

"Nay, I canna. I must see that ye are safe first."

"Then at least let me run, I couldn't bear it if I stole any strength ye needed."

"I've plenty of it." He managed to smile and wink at her in a way that made her belly flip, and warm heat rush to her face.

Even with imminent danger, Rory made her feel like she was the only one in the world.

Moira wrapped her arms around his neck and smiled back. "Ye are unique, Rory. An amazing man with boundless compassion."

He grunted.

By the time they reached the castle, Logan and Ewan were at the top of the barbican, watching those on the other side of the gate. They motioned to Rory.

"Will ye be all right now?" he asked.

"Yes. I see Shona and Emma on the steps."

The two women wore equal expressions of concern standing just outside the castle doors.

Rory pressed a kiss to her forehead when he set her down. She closed her eyes a moment, her hands squeezing his upper arms. There were so many things she wanted to say to him and not nearly enough time in which to do it.

"I'll speak with ye soon," he said.

She dipped her head. "Good luck."

Moira watched him climb the stairs to the battlements, where he joined the men, regretting that she'd not just come out with how she felt. Had just leapt from the ridge and told him she still loved him.

From here, the way he stiffened his back, she could tell that whoever was below was not someone he wanted to see. One guess, she'd say it was MacLeod. Lifting the hem of her skirts, she hurried up the castle front stairs to stand with Emma and Shona.

"Who is it?" she asked hesitantly.

"Ranulf MacLeod." Emma's response confirmed Moira's fears.

She shivered, hugging herself. "What does he want?"

"Rory," Shona whispered.

"Logan will protect him," Emma said.

Moira kept her gaze on Rory and the men, they were shouting to those on the other side of the gate, the answering call lost to her ears at this distance.

"Open the gates!" Logan shouted.

"Protect him?" Moira said, panicked. "He just invited the enemy inside!"

## RORY

"I'm not certain this is a good idea. MacLeod could try to take a shot at ye, Rory," Logan said. "Ye'll need to be on your guard."

"Aye." Rory clenched and unclenched his fists at his sides. "Ye've done the right thing; the best thing for me to do is to talk to him. Perhaps with ye as a mediator he will be more understanding."

The men descended the stairs as the gates were opened and the clopping of horses' hooves was heard in the bailey below. Rory caught sight of Moira on the stairs. She was hugging herself, worry written all over her face. He wished more than anything to rush over to her and offer comfort, but he couldn't. Their gazes locked and he quirked a smile, hoping that small gesture would settle her nerves.

She smiled tentatively back and he mouthed the words: *It's going to be all right.*

And it damned well better be.

"Shouldn't the women go inside?" Rory asked.

"Aye," Logan said, turning to Gregor, one of the guards

walking with them. "Escort them inside. Tell my wife I'll be along shortly to speak with her."

Gregor nodded, though his face paled slightly. If Rory had to guess, Lady Emma didn't much like being told what to do, and was likely to give the poor guard a hard time.

Rory chanced a glance toward the women and could have laughed at Logan's expense, but the situation left him feeling so tense he barely smiled. Lady Emma was shaking her head, hands on her hips, looking as though she was about to give a piece of her mind to Gregor. The man uttered something softly and her hands dropped. She nodded then encouraged Shona and Moira to go inside, too. Easier than Rory had guessed. Perhaps because of the other two women present.

Rory stepped off the last stair and came face to face with his son. He halted, breath caught. Damn, but it was like beholding himself fifteen years ago.

"Rory MacLeod," Ranulf said. "I've been looking for ye."

"I've only just returned, and heard of it." Rory kept his voice calm and void of any emotion.

"Why have ye been hiding for all these years?" Ranulf slid from his horse, sauntering within a few feet of Rory.

Ballocks. He'd not expected the sudden crush of emotions tunneling through his limbs. Overwhelmed, he dragged in a breath. "Ye've grown up," he managed.

"Traitor," Ranulf seethed.

Rory shook his head. "I'm no traitor."

Ranulf puffed his chest, his cheeks ruddy from anger. "Ye will address me as Laird."

"Ye're not the only laird present, 'twould be rude of me." Rory couldn't help the jibe. The lad was obstinate, and try as he might to be civil, Ranulf was not cooperating.

"I *am* your laird." Ranulf's eyes skated to his guards. "And I deserve your show of loyalty afore I bring ye to justice for what ye did."

"Let us speak privately." Rory tried to walk around Ranulf, but the young buck was not interested in talking, he'd come for a fight.

And Rory knew it, for a certainty, the moment the tip of a blade touched his spine. The sound of at least a dozen or more swords being drawn from their scabbards followed. MacLeods and Grants, all with weapons drawn.

"Dinna do it," Logan said. "I've welcomed ye into my gates and I'd hate to toss ye out afore we've had a chance to talk."

"Toss me out with this vermin," Ranulf demanded, the tip of his blade pressing a little harder to Rory's back.

"I'm afraid I canna do that. Ye see, I've offered Rory my protection."

"Ye, the Guardian of Scotland, would offer protection to a murderer?" Ranulf sounded put out, the venom in his tone thick.

"He's no murderer, and ye know it," Logan said. "Drop your weapon. Let us go inside."

"Nay," Rory hollered.

"If ye dinna drop your weapon, I will order my men to take your men down, and then I'll be forced to take ye down. I have the power to do so, but it is not a power I wish to wield." Logan had remained calm throughout his speech, but the undercurrent of his tone brooked no argument.

Rory raised his hands in the air, showing he held no weapons, and slowly turned around. Ranulf didn't move, his blade only sliding over Rory's ribs and pressing against his chest.

Looking his son in the eyes, Rory said, "The lad does not want to talk, my laird. He wants to fight. I shall give him what he wants."

Logan didn't argue. From his periphery, Rory could see

the man gave a curt nod, but what he was really staring at was Ranulf, and the way he fumed even more at being called a lad.

"I dinna just want a fight. I want ye dead!"

Rory grinned, though it was more of a grimace. "I know it."

"Ye murdered my parents."

Rory shook his head.

"Ye left our clan to die." Ranulf would most likely run through his list of accusations.

"If there is one thing I'm guilty of, 'tis running when I should have stayed. But look what it got ye. Ye're the laird now."

Ranulf's eyes turned dark with hatred, his lips curled. The men that stood around them simply looked from Ranulf to Rory and back again. Many of them were young, they wouldn't remember that Rory was the nephew of the late laird, and they definitely wouldn't know that Ranulf was Rory's son.

"Of course *I'm* the laird. Who else would be? Certainly not *ye*."

Rory put the flat of his hand on top of Ranulf's sword and slowly pushed it down. "I've never wanted to be laird."

"And ye canna!" The lad sounded positively irate.

"A blessing."

"A blessing?" Ranulf sounded exasperated, letting out a short bark of laughter. "Have ye lost your mind?"

"Nay. 'Tis a blessing ye were left alive. I thank the stars every night that ye and the other children were taken to safety."

"But ye *abandoned* us." Ranulf raised his sword once more.

"For your own good."

Again, he laughed. "Ye know nothing of what is good for me."

"Ye may be right about that. I'm happy to give ye the fight

ye want, Ranulf, but let us do it like men. No weapons. We'll use our bare hands."

"I will bludgeon ye to death." Ranulf jerked the blade, and Rory yanked away in enough time that it didn't pierce his skin.

"So ye say. I'll not be killing ye today."

Ranulf turned another shade of red. Seemed that every word Rory uttered made the lad angrier and angrier.

"Because I'm going to kill *ye*."

"I'm afraid I will not allow that, either."

Ranulf threw his sword to the ground. "Ye should have died. Ye should have been the one left to bleed into the earth."

## ✨ 16 ✨
### MOIRA

Standing in Emma's solar, hands clutching the sill of the stone window, Moira vied for viewing space in the center the other two women.

She was also experiencing what she thought could have very well been a panic attack.

Her palms were sweaty; knees were locked. She was light-headed, hot but also cold. Her teeth chattered, so she kept them tightly clamped, which was not only giving her a headache, but she couldn't draw a decent breath. Her heart beat so fast, she was certain it echoed through the window to sound like thunder in the clouds.

"Why is he doing this?" She spoke the words, but she didn't really expect an answer, and both Emma and Shona seemed to know that.

The two of them simply placed their hands over hers, keeping her anchored, their presence holding her upright when she wasn't certain she had the strength the stand on her own.

Ranulf's sword skittered across the bailey grounds when he tossed it. He and Rory had divested themselves of their weapons, a pile of metal glinting in the sun by several guards' feet. Their fists were raised and they walked in a circle, assessing one another.

Question after question stormed Moira's mind, but she refused to pay any of them attention. Refused to take her mind off of Rory and what was happening below, other than to whisper a prayer up to the sky to keep him safe. She might not have been from this century, but she knew a murderous look when she saw one and Ranulf, Laird of MacLeod, had murder in his eyes.

Rory on the other hand, didn't look at all disturbed. He looked resigned. As if this were a chore, he'd known he'd needed to complete, like when she had to do her laundry on Sunday night, and then, inevitably fold it when it was finished.

But this wasn't laundry, this was a brawl. This was a duel, and if movies were going to serve her now, they wouldn't simply punch each other a couple of times. There would be no rules, and Ranulf could kill Rory.

"Rory has the advantage," Shona murmured. "He is a seasoned warrior."

*Seasoned*. Made him sound like a hunk of beef. Moira tasted blood on her tongue, realizing too late how hard she'd been biting the inside of her cheek. "But Ranulf is younger, more agile. How can Rory compete with that?"

"Age and agility won't necessarily trump skill and experience," Emma said, she graced Moira with a gentle smile and squeezed her hand. "Physically, Rory can win. It's the mental side I'm worried about."

"Mental?"

Emma nodded. "Your Rory believes he deserves this. He's a man of honor and men of honor always take their punishment."

The first punch was thrown, and not by Rory. Ranulf flung

out his fist—and Rory just stood there, letting the young laird hit him right on the cheek. The sound of his knuckles hitting flesh cracked through the bailey, ricocheting up the side of the castle and into the window.

Moira shuddered, her cheek feeling phantom pains from that punch.

Rory remained still, his head barely moved even with the force of the blow. Ranulf took his chance, wrenching back his fist and letting another crack fly. Again, Rory was still, but this time Ranulf's fist hit against his lip, splitting it, and a small amount of blood dribbled down Rory's chin.

Moira's heart lurched. She wanted to fly down the stairs and into the courtyard. To tell the two of them to grow up, that men didn't behave this way.

"Do something." Moira nervously tapped her booted feet on the wood-planked floor, her fingers digging into the stone. "Move."

Emma disappeared for a moment, returning with a glass of strong-smelling whisky. "Drink."

Moira wrinkled her nose. "I can't. It smells horrible."

"It will ease your anxiety. Just a little sip at a time."

"Maybe ye shouldn't watch." Shona looked very concerned. "I won't watch either. We can go read a book."

Moira gave her sister a look that said *over my dead body*. As painful as it was to watch Rory get beat up by the overgrown brat, it would hurt worse not to know what was happening. She took a sip of the whisky, feeling a raw burn edge its way down her throat, and kept on watching.

Rory let Ranulf get in another rough hit, which opened up a cut on his brow, before he caught the man's fist in one hand, holding him still. When Ranulf couldn't get free, he swung his opposite fist, only to be caught by Rory again. Rory leaned close, his large hands swarming Ranulf's smaller fists, and murmured something in Ranulf's face that she couldn't quite hear.

"Killing ye will solve everything!" The brat's bellowed response gave her at least some indication of the conversation.

At a minimum, it was reassuring to know that Rory didn't think fighting or killing was the answer. He might have been from the sixteenth century, but it appeared the man had good sense.

Moira gazed from Ewan to Logan. Why did neither of them step in? Why did no one try to convince MacLeod this was wrong? All the men below, Logan and Ewan included, simply stood by, stone-faced, watching as blood poured from Rory's face and MacLeod struggled to unlock himself from Rory's grip.

There was a certain measured control within Rory. A power that he held in check, that MacLeod should fear if it became unleashed, but the young laird did not seem to notice, and no one warned him either.

"Get off me, ye coward," Ranulf shouted, still fighting against Rory's hold. "Ye shamed my mother!"

What? Shamed his mother? Moira stared at Rory, willing him to answer, so she could know what that possibly meant.

Rory did let go at MacLeod's words, giving a slight shove against the young man's unleashed hands, which caused Ranulf to stumble backward. Still, his expression stricken, Rory did not advance.

"I cared for her, ye know, Ranulf. I did." His lips were pressed in a firm line, sadness in the creases of his eyes.

"Bastard!" Ranulf flew at him, but this time, Rory dodged him and stuck out a leg, tripping the overeager, furious, laird.

Words spoken of a past woman, Ranulf's mother, seemed to have woken *Moira's* Rory to finally take the brat in hand. What had happened? Did Rory mourn her when she died?

Did he mourn her still? Was it love? He said he cared for her. He had to have loved her. Rory wasn't capable of anything less. She'd never experienced such love as she had with him. Intense. Heated. Full of amazement.

Tears sprung to Moira's eyes at the thought of Rory having loved another, though it must have been a long time ago, before he met her. The way it felt as though a cold, gauntleted hand squeezed around her heart, spoke volumes.

Moira didn't want to let him go. Didn't want him to love another. *She* loved *him*. He was supposed to be hers. And he'd offered her his love and, though she desperately wanted to take it, she'd shunned him.

This was all wrong. He was hers and she was his. She couldn't go on without telling him how she felt, especially if he were to be murdered, beaten to death, by the puny MacLeod.

Moira chugged the rest of the whisky and then whirled from the window, prepared to enter the bailey and shout just how she felt, that the fighting had to end, but both Emma and Shona held onto her.

"Ye cannot," Shona whispered.

"I have to."

Emma shook her head. "It is not like modern times. You will not be welcomed. You will be removed. Forcefully. Trust me. It's happened to me before."

"I have been carried over Ewan's shoulder enough times to know that this is true," Shona added.

"Like a sack of potatoes?" Moira managed, then she was lurching back to the window. If she couldn't be down there with him, than at least he could know she was there, watching from above.

Rory had the young laird pinned to the ground on his stomach, hands behind his back, while he knelt on the base of Ranulf's spine, keeping him restrained.

"Ye shame your mother with your vile words. Ye shame your clan and your own verra existence." Rory's bellow could be heard as clearly as though he was in the room. "Your laird would not be proud of ye in this moment."

"My laird is dead because of *ye*."

"Nay, lad. Your laird is dead because of *ye*."

There was a collective gasp in the crowd.

"Lies! Lies ye spill." Ranulf writhed beneath Rory's hold, working frantically to get free.

Fury consumed Rory's countenance. "Damn ye, lad! If ye'd not been off shagging the Mackenzie's daughter they'd not have come seeking war!"

Suddenly, Ranulf stopped fighting. He remained so still, Moira thought he might have passed out from the pressure of Rory's hold. But then he said something she couldn't quite catch, and Rory nodded.

"There is so much more to this than we can hear up here," Emma muttered. "Maybe we should go down to listen."

"What?" Moira gaped at her. "Ye just said we'd be removed."

"Not if we hide well enough." Emma winked. "I should have thought of that sooner. Pregnancy brain. There is a balistraria alcove by the front doors where guards can sit with their bows swords to injure anyone trying to break through. It will give us a great view of the bailey—and the sound will be infinitely better."

They hurried down the stairs, but not too fast for Emma's pregnant shape, quickly locating the recess. They peered through the cross-shaped opening to see that Rory stood with Ranulf before him looking utterly dejected. The men of the MacLeod clan had all knelt, their hands over their heart.

"What's happening?" Moira asked.

"It looks like they are pledging their loyalty to Rory," Shona mused.

"But why?" Moira asked.

Emma shook her head. "I don't know."

But soon, they had their answer as the men began to chant to Rory, their "rightful laird."

"How is that possible?" Moira asked no one in particular.

Ranulf did not bow. He seethed. He jostled past the men, grabbing his sword from the ground, his intent obvious. But he didn't make it more than six inches before finding several blades at his throat.

"Ye'll not get away with usurping me!" Ranulf shouted. "I dinna care who ye are! Ye'll never be my laird, or my father! I hate ye! I loathe the verra ground ye walk on, the air ye breathe and with every last breath of my body, I will see ye dead!" His outburst over, Ranulf fled through the gates.

Rory started to go after him, but Logan held a hand to his chest, murmuring what sounded like, *Let him go.*

Moira leaned back against the wall. Her heart pounding. Hands pressed to her face, uncertain she'd heard correctly. Mind whirling. Shock made her dizzy. "Did MacLeod say *father?*"

Emma and Shona both nodded at the same time, their eyes as wide as Moira's felt.

"Rory has a son."

## RORY

Watching his son storm through the gates tore at Rory's chest. He wanted to race after him, to make him see reason, but Ranulf was beyond sense at the moment.

Rory had never meant for any of their past to come out, but the lad, when he started to berate his dear mother, that was the last straw for Rory. His mother had never done anything to harm the lad, only spoiled him rotten, as was her want.

Ranulf's rage had only blown to the surface more when the men realized Rory was their rightful laird and had bent to their knees to pledge their loyalty to him. HI son had told them nay, had shouted it, but still they rested. They could not support a lad like Ranulf, so bent on hatred and revenge, and so obviously in pain that he was lacking in judgment. There were also the tiny matters of the lairdship being Rory's in truth, and Ranulf's adolescent lust that brought war to the MacLeod's doorstep in the first place.

Rory would accept the title if need be, but only until Ranulf was ready to take the position himself.

"Follow him," Rory said to several of the guards. "Make sure he does not do anything rash."

The men nodded and hurried to catch up.

"I think that could have gone better," Logan said, sarcasm leaping from his words.

Rory crossed his arms over his chest, staring at the cloud of dust following in Ranulf's wake. "Ye think?"

Ewan clapped Rory on the back. "He'll return. As soon as he's licked his wounds."

"I dinna think so." Rory had seen the hatred in his son's eyes. "I believe him. He'll not rest until I'm dead."

"Temper-filled words, nothing more," Logan said.

Rory swiped at his face, blood coming away on his palm. "I'm not so certain. I do not deserve this position. It is his and he has held it for many years. How could I take something from my own flesh and blood?"

"When your flesh and blood wants to kill ye?" Logan shrugged. "I'm not a Da yet, and I know ye've not quite considered yourself one, but it is the duty of every parent to lead their children toward their best self. He has been lacking in leadership. If ye owe him anything, it is that."

"He's a grown man."

"Not quite." Logan chuckled. "How old is he?"

"Nineteen last month."

"Ye see, he's practically still a pup."

Rory chuckled. "I was a Da at that age."

"Ye're the exception."

Rory let out a low growl of frustration.

"Come inside and get cleaned up. Looks like ye could use a few stitches above the eye. Why'd ye stand there like a fool and let him hit ye?" Logan asked.

"I felt he deserved that much. Would have let him hit me a few more times if he'd not brought up his mother." *Poor Abi.*

Rory started for the keep, intent on seeking Moira's healing touch. As he topped the stairs, the main door flung open and she was throwing herself into his arms.

"Thank god ye're all right!" She pressed her tear-stained face to his chest, and Rory held her tight in his embrace.

"I'm all right, I swear it."

She pulled back, hands clasped to his upper arms. "Ye're bleeding something fierce. Best let me clean ye up."

Rory grinned. "How funny we are right back to the beginning."

"The beginning?" Ewan asked.

Rory ran his finger along her jawline, his gaze locked on hers. "Aye. The first time she met me I was pretty torn up from the battle for which Ranulf wants me dead."

"So when ye say ye ran, ye ran to the future?"

"I suppose so."

"And when ye came back?"

"I didna know how long I'd been gone. Felt it best to start anew. Besides, I was trying to figure out a way to get back to Moira when her sister showed up. My duty was to her, to her sister, and I couldna risk going back to my clan."

"Enough talk, let's get ye cleaned up." Moira grabbed his

hand and started to lead him into the great hall, but Rory shook his head. "What?"

"Upstairs. I need some quiet to think."

"All right." She led him up the stairs to the chamber they'd been given to share, but had yet to do so. "Shona will be back soon with some salve for your wounds."

She went over to the washbasin and soaked a cloth, bringing it back toward him. "Sit down," she ordered, shoving him toward a chair.

Rory did as she bade, trying not to wince when the cold cloth touched the searing cuts on his face as she cleaned away the blood. He knew she must have questions, and he wanted to give her answers.

"Moira, when we were on the shore, I told ye I needed to tell ye something."

"Shh..." she said. "There's no need to talk about it just yet. Let's get ye—"

Rory shook his head, pulled both of her hands tenderly from his face. "I need to tell ye now. I've put it off long enough. I should have told ye from the beginning." He kissed her knuckles. "I have a son."

She nodded, but didn't say anything, allowing him to finish. He told her the same thing he'd told Logan, about his uncle's wife, Abi. Their deaths. His guilt.

"I was young, and thought myself in love. It wasn't until I met ye that I knew what real love was."

"Rory..." Tears came to her eyes and before she could wipe them away, he cupped her face and leaned forward, kissing away her sorrow.

"I'm sorry, love. I should have told ye."

"Ye dinna need to be sorry. I could never hold your past against ye, or the fact that ye loved another and had a child. This is your life. Ranulf and Abi are a part of that life. I love ye and I'm sorry it took me so long to tell ye. When I saw ye fighting, and I thought I might lose ye"—He made a disgruntled noise at that notion—"I couldn't bear it. I wanted to run to ye, to fling open the doors and demand Ranulf stop. I nearly did it, too."

Rory chuckled. "Ye're a fierce, lass. One of the many reasons I love ye." He tugged her forward, pressing his lips to hers, wincing at the pain of his cut.

She gently pulled back and dabbed at his bloody lip. "Don't make me hurt ye more."

"But a kiss, *that* hurts *so* good."

She giggled. "Even with a bloody, cut up face ye think of flirting."

"And kissing."

She leaned forward and kissed him gently on the side of his mouth that was not wounded. "Good thing I've got the healing touch."

"Och, love, ye'll have me undone."

## ✷ 17 ✷
### SHONA

"I think ye need to tell her." Shona rubbed her husband's shoulders while he took his boots off in their chamber.

After the MacLeod men had given their allegiance to Rory, Ewan had to work with the Grant men to make certain the walls were safe as well as the inside in case it was a hoax of some sort.

Ranulf had yet to reappear. The men sent after him had returned, saying they'd lost his trail fifteen miles north.

Ewan sighed. "I know."

"Emma will be relieved to know that her beliefs all these years were true."

"Aye." He cleared his throat, tossing his boots a few feet away, thudding against the wardrobe. Taking her arms, he tugged her around to sit in his lap. "There is something I need to tell ye."

Shona stroked the creases on his forehead. "Ye frown too much," she teased.

"My name is Troy."

Shona's smile faded, her belly feeling as though it had flopped somewhere on the floor. "What?"

"I didna remember until we ended up in the present. Until then, I've always thought my name was Ewan. I didna know how to tell ye. But if I confess to Emma, she'll know my name, and I think ye, my wife, should know all. Ewan is not my real name."

Shona swallowed around the bone-dry lump in her throat. "Is there anything else ye haven't told me?"

"Nay, love."

That was a relief at least she tried to reason in her shock at finding out her husband had a completely different name. "Why do ye call yourself Ewan if 'tis not your true name?"

"When I came here the first time, I pulled myself from the loch, fell unconscious beneath a yew tree. The elder crofters that found me and brought me to Gealach called me Ewan because of it. The name stuck."

"Which do ye prefer, husband?" she whispered. "I shall call ye whatever ye wish."

"I am Ewan. I might have been Troy as a boy, but I barely remember that life. I've forged an existence here, and Ewan is who I am."

Shona kissed his wrinkled brow, working to smooth the creases with her thumb. "Ye look like an Ewan to me."

"What exactly does an Ewan look like?"

"Tall. Handsome. Fierce. Sexy as hell."

"And a cock the size—"

Shona cut him off with a bite to his lower lip. "A cock the perfect size to pleasure his *wife*."

Ewan chuckled. "Still thinking of Hildie, are ye?"

Shona let out an exasperated half-sigh, half-laugh. "Hildie has nothing on me."

"Never were there truer words spoken."

Shona was reminded of the ointments aging on her work-table. As soon as they'd returned to Gealach, she had begun her search for herbs and fungi to recreate an antibiotic for

Hildie and her ladies. She hoped to have it done within a few months. But for the time being, she'd much rather make love to her husband.

"Take me to bed, Ewan."

## RORY

UNABLE TO SLEEP, RORY SNUCK FROM MOIRA'S ROOM where she'd let him sleep, holding her—and though he'd wanted to desperately, he'd not tried to make love to her, in hopes his restraint would help to further gain her trust.

The night sky was quickly fading with the rising sun. The bailey was empty save for a few guards standing watch. He nodded to them and then trudged toward the stairs that led to the top of the gate tower and the rest of the battlements. The crisp air felt good on his skin, warding off some of the sting of his wounds. He'd refused to drink much of the whisky he'd been offered, as well as the tincture Shona had tried to get him to drink to help him sleep.

He had to keep his wits about him. Everything was happening so fast and if Ranulf returned, his *son*, he had to be able to speak to him without liquor dulling his senses. Over the ramparts, the sun was slowly being revealed. The guards nodded to him and then returned to their duties, gazing out over the loch and marsh beyond.

Rory walked the length of the battlements, and then leaned against the stone. Damn but he had a headache. One eye was half swollen shut. His lip hurt like hell. Moving his jaw sent pain shooting down his neck. Ranulf might not have yet had the strength and skill of Rory, but he was halfway there, and he could land one hell of a punch.

"Couldn't sleep?" Ewan wandered up beside him.

"Nay."

"Me either."

Rory grunted.

They stayed beside each other, quiet, each leaning against the crenellations and watching the world wake up.

"Shite." Ewan slapped the stone.

Rory jerked his gaze toward the direction Ewan stared. "Ballocks! Where the hell did he find *them?*"

Riding across the marsh was his son and perhaps fifty men wearing MacDonald colors.

The horn sounded, and Ewan disappeared in a blur of plaid as he ran across the battlements issuing orders. They would soon be under attack. It appeared Ranulf's hatred ran deeper than Rory anticipated. Only a man in desperate need of revenge would bring an army of the enemy to an ally's door.

Rory had to put a stop to this. He couldn't allow anyone else to be hurt because his son was holding a grudge. Rory ran for the nearest stairs, took them three at a time and hurried to the stable. He readied his horse in record time and galloped to the gate.

"Let me out. I'm going to settle this now."

"I canna open the gate," Taig shouted down.

"Open the bloody gate!"

"Nay, Laird MacLeod, I canna."

Rory's blood boiled. "Open the gate or I'll come up there, chop off your ballocks and make ye swallow them."

"I mean no offense, my laird, but if I open the gates, my own laird will do worse to me than making me eat my own ballocks."

Rory let out a frustrated bellow.

"Rory MacLeod!" The roar came from beyond the wall. His son. Calling for him.

"Let me out," Rory growled at Taig.

"Nay, man, I canna."

Rory was ready to pummel the man—any man really—to the ground. He jumped from his horse and climbed the stairs to the gate tower, peering down at his son who smirked with righteousness.

"What's this about, Ranulf?" Rory demanded.

"Getting back what ye stole from me."

"I've stolen nothing."

Ranulf glanced at MacDonald and whispered something that Rory could not hear.

Logan stepped onto the battlements, placing himself beside Rory—showing they were allies. "MacDonald. Ye're not welcome here. We warned ye that if ye came back the only way ye'd be leaving was in pieces."

MacDonald laughed. "I think not."

"So assured ye are." Logan grinned, it was malicious, hungry. The man looked ready to do battle and to tear MacDonald to pieces with his bare hands.

MacDonald made a tsking noise. "We've come for Rory MacLeod. Toss him down, or let him out the gates and I'll be on my way."

"I do not take commands from traitors." Logan's voice was steady, not revealing a single emotion.

"Then perhaps ye'd take the order from your young queen."

Rory raised a brow. An order from the infant queen was laughable.

"Who have ye made an alliance with?" Logan's brow furrowed. "Did they know they were signing a contract with the devil himself?"

"The regent and I go a long way back."

"The regent has no use for Rory, and if he wants him, he can come tell me himself."

MacDonald laughed, low in his throat. "'Tis not only Rory

the regent wants. I'm his representative and if ye will not heed his demands, then I am to forcibly take ye to Edinburgh."

"I was just in Edinburgh. He mentioned no such summons."

"'Tis new."

"Lies," Logan said under his breath. "Prepare the archers," he demanded.

"Ye're a dead man," MacDonald shouted.

"Grant, dinna do this," Rory said. "Just let me go. I'll not be responsible for more deaths."

"MacDonald will try to fight no matter what. If ye went down there, he'd simply demand something else."

"What is happening?" Emma's voice reached them both, and standing beside her were Shona and Moira.

"What are ye doing up here, woman? Go back inside, else ye birth the bairn in the middle of a battle." Logan's exasperation showed on his face and his stance. He looked ready to nock her in a bow and shoot her back to her chamber.

"Another battle?" Emma asked, disappointment clear. "Why won't that whoreson just leave us alone?"

"Go back inside," Logan's voice was strained. "Please."

"Grant!" MacDonald bellowed.

"Prepare for battle!" Logan answered, turning his attention back to MacDonald.

"Who are they?" MacDonald roared, his sword drawn and pointed at the lassies.

Ranulf leaned over and whispered to MacDonald once more.

Rory had been so intent on the men below he'd not taken notice of Moira peering over the side with Shona trying to yank her back.

"Get them down!" Rory yelled rushing forward, attempting to hide Shona and Moira with his body.

Ewan was right behind him.

"One of red and one of black, born at Ayreshire and swept back, lost forever the princesses of time, the last of the king's most sacred line." All fell silent as MacDonald repeated the nursery rhyme they'd heard since childhood. "So it is true."

Rory met Moira's gaze. "Inside. Now."

She nodded, fear in her eyes. "I'm sorry. I just wanted to see..."

"'Tis too dangerous. Please..."

All three of the women were rushed inside, guards flanking them.

"Rubbish," Logan said. "Ye're a fool to believe a childhood rhyme upon seeing two women."

"There is magic here, Grant, and ye know it. I know it. Give them to me and ye can keep Rory."

"Nay!" Ranulf shouted.

Logan bared his teeth. "Ye'll be getting no one behind these walls." He turned to his archers. "Ready your bows!"

"Shields!" MacDonald ordered.

The click of arrows being nocked, the stretch of bowstrings, and the scrape of shields being raised echoed in the deafening silence.

"I canna let ye do this!" Rory hissed. "Grant, please. He's my son."

"Your son sided with the enemy. An enemy who demands death. This has been a long time coming." Logan grimaced, his eyes alive with fire. "MacDonald and I, we were born to wage war."

MacDonald and his men began to retreat, their horses walking steadily backward. Rory prayed his son, as hateful and vengeful as he was, got the hell out of the way.

Logan ticked off numbers in his head, a countdown, tapping his fingers methodically on the stone.

"Fire!"

Arrows sang through the air, arching up to touch the clouds before sailing down toward the enemy.

Relief swept through Rory when most of the arrows sank into the ground, a few into shields, only a couple into the thighs and arms of the warriors below—and Ranulf was left uninjured.

MacDonald called for the men to retreat at the same time Logan shouted for his archers to reload.

"They'll be back," Logan growled.

Rory glowered at the laird, crossing his arms over his chest. "This can all be easily settled with me."

"Nay, it canna. MacDonald wants power. All he needed was an excuse to come back here, and Ranulf gave him one. If he's aligned himself with the regent then he is no doubt trying to convince the regent that he should be Guardian of Scotland and not myself."

"Then MacDonald would have no need for Ranulf. He's expendable." Rory dragged a hand through his hair.

"An excuse."

"Well, even if he is a bastard backstabber, the lad is my son, though I was never his father. I'll not let him get himself killed by your enemy."

"Your enemy, too, MacLeod," Logan growled. "He's come here for your woman under the pretense that she's an Ayreshire princess."

Rory seethed. "She is an Ayreshire."

"But we dinna know for a certainty, if she's actually one of them. Could all be a huge coincidence."

"Dammit, Logan. Let me go and reason with Ranulf." Rory clenched his fists at his sides.

Logan eyed him wearily. "Reasoning with him will not stop this battle from happening."

"But it might just save his life."

Logan held up his hands. "If ye want to get yourself killed, then by all means. Do so."

Rory stormed passed Logan and down the stairs. He called for the dozen men he had to his name—men he wasn't even certain would stand behind him when it came down to it—who mounted up behind him. The gates were opened just enough for them to file out. A dozen against fifty wasn't good odds even with men as skilled as Rory, and especially not with these men.

"Rory!" The shout was from Moira from an upper window.

"I love ye, lass," he whispered, a slight wave of his hand, hoping she would see his mouthed words.

"Wait," Ewan called.

Rory stilled his horse only long enough to see that Ewan was joining him with two-dozen men.

"What are ye doing?" Rory asked.

"This ends now," Ewan said.

"Nay." Rory reined in his horse, cutting off Ewan's progress. "Ye and your men are supposed to stay inside. To protect the castle and its treasure, just as ye always have."

"Logan's orders." Ewan's stare dared Rory to challenge him.

Logan appeared, then, on horseback, another two-dozen men behind him. "We stand together. We're bound, whether we like it or not." He grinned, showing Rory he wasn't disappointed in the prospect.

Rory bowed briefly on his horse. "I pledged my allegiance to ye, not the other way around."

"No need to bow to me, Laird MacLeod. We'll call this the point at which we formed an official alliance between Clan Grant and Clan MacLeod."

Rory held out his arm and Logan gripped it. "Agreed."

They made formations on horseback outside of the gates.

Logan allowed Rory to be first in line at his own request, followed by Logan and his men, and Ewan's elite forces.

MacDonald had made his formations, too. The bastard sat at the back and was sending Ranulf out in the first.

"Dinna kill my son," Rory said, the order passed back amongst the troops. "Knock him out if ye have to, but he is to be taken alive."

Rory raised his sword in the air and issued a battle cry that shook the heavens. Ewan was right; this was going to end now. He was tired of hiding. Tired of running. He'd not be able to live out the rest of his days looking over his shoulder at an enemy vowing revenge. Nay, he'd look him straight in the eye—right now.

His sword sang through the air as he swished it down, giving the order to, "Attack!"

They charged on their horses, leaning over the withers, shields raised, swords steady. Beneath him, Rory's borrowed mount moved with grace and power. He charged Ranulf, intent on being the one to take him prisoner. A split second later, he was clashing with one of the MacDonald men who intercepted, knocking his horse into Ranulf's and shoving him aside. Ranulf looked ready to topple over but righted himself in time to attack one of what used to be his own men, while Rory engaged with the interferer.

The MacDonald warrior fought like a vicious bear, stabbing with a long, curved dagger and slicing with his sword, but Rory blocked each blow, though his attention wasn't in it. He couldn't stop watching his son to see if the men followed his orders not to kill him, for Ranulf was intent on carnage.

Rory dispatched of the MacDonald warrior, only to be attacked by another. He bent backward, dodging a hacking blow of an axe, only to feel the slice of some other blade in his shoulder. The wound stung, but it wouldn't slow him down. Rory thundered his anger and brought his own sword arching down on the warrior, reaching back to stab another who tried to pounce on him.

Sweat dripped from his brow and he swiped it with the back of his arm, his already bruised face throbbing. He searched the sea of brutal warriors for his son. Ranulf was still holding his own, and though Rory shouldn't have been impressed because that meant he was hurting Rory's own men, a part of him was. He whirled his horse in his son's direction.

"Ranulf! Ye're mine!" he bellowed.

Ranulf flicked his gaze in Rory's direction, an abrupt enough shift in his attention that the warrior he'd been fighting—one of Ewan's men—was able to hit him on the temple with the hilt of his sword. Rory reached his side as Ranulf's eyes slid into the back of his head and he slipped from the saddle.

"Good work," Rory said to the man he'd been fighting. "Baodan?"

"Aye, my laird."

"Take him back to the castle." Rory maneuvered his son's bulk to Baodan's lap, and slapped the man's horse on the rump, sending him in a gallop toward the gates.

The Grant and MacLeod men, seeing that Ranulf had been obtained, blocked the path of all the MacDonald men trying to get in the way.

Satisfied that his son would be safely behind walls, Rory searched out MacDonald, meeting Ewan and Logan in the center of the battlefield.

"There!" Rory shouted, pointing toward a lone figure racing across the moors.

"We canna let him get away," Logan said.

"We end this," Ewan declared.

Rory had a sudden flashback to years before, a similar scene. Nay. He couldn't let them go, but they were already racing forward and if he didn't join them, then he'd not be able to help them should MacDonald prove his treachery once more.

Several MacDonald warriors broke away from the melee in pursuit of their master, hot on the heels of Ewan and Logan, their swords raised and ready to attack.

"Nay!" Rory bellowed.

He'd not let this happen again.

## ❦ 18 ❦

### RORY

Rory hurtled forward, his blood thick with battle-rage. He gained on the men following his friends, blades of grass disappearing foot by foot until, finally, he was upon them. With a resounding battle cry, he raised his sword bringing it down on one warrior, causing the others to turn around and raise their blades.

Rory yanked his second sword from his scabbard, one in each hand. His vision was blinded by red, and all he could do was block and thrust. There were six of them surrounding him, and he decided that even if he died right here and now, at least he'd die protecting his allies, his son and the woman he loved—the latter two safe behind the castle walls.

Every move seemed to be in slow motion. The sounds slurred, the gentle breeze so ironic considering their ruthless fight to survive. As he hacked at the men—one down five to go—their blades sliced into his own limbs. Slice. Cut. Arc. Swipe. Twist. Every move he'd ever known was brought out in this battle of might.

He was startled by the sudden fall from their horses of two opponents.

Ewan and Logan.

They'd turned around and now dispatched of the MacDonald warriors surrounding Rory.

With renewed vigor, Rory took out another, who'd nearly stabbed Logan in the back. What felt like seconds later, all six of the MacDonald warriors littered the ground.

"Laird MacDonald," Rory said, breathless. "He's gotten away."

"Let him go." Logan swiped at his brow. "He'll be back, we know it. And we'll be waiting for him."

"We need to get ye back to the castle. Ye're going to need more stitches." Ewan studied the cuts on Rory's limbs. "That one is looking particularly deep." He pointed to Rory's shoulder.

Rory nodded, his tongue feeling a little thick, his limbs slightly trembling. His grip wasn't as tight anymore either. Both swords were harder to hold with his palms slickened with blood. One fell to the ground, and then the other, making a subtle thud against the bloodstained grass.

Battle-lust had been what kept him conscience in the wake of having lost so much blood.

As soon as he started to slip from the saddle, Ewan caught him, setting him upright.

"Let's go. I'll get your weapons," Ewan said. "Hold on tight."

"I can ride." Rory widened his eyes, blinking, as tiny black dots started to appear. He could ride. He could. Blurred vision be damned.

He nudged his horse forward. Logan rode up beside him, keeping pace, perhaps just a tad worried that Rory might fall from the horse.

They crossed under the gate without incident, for which Rory thanked the Lord and Fate for watching out for him.

They might have lost MacDonald, but there were so many other wins to be grateful for.

"Rory!" Moira screamed.

He tried to look for her, but by now his vision was gone completely and he was feeling light and heavy all at once. "Moira." He tried to say her name, formed the syllables on his tongue, but he couldn't hear them. Wasn't sure if she did either. "Moira, my love." Again, he swore he spoke.

"Ohmygod," Moira said.

Rory smiled. He could smell her, that spicy citrus scent that was all her own. God, how he loved her. He would miss her most of all if he left this earth right now. They'd never even gotten the chance to rekindle their love.

"I will love ye, forever, *mo chridhe*," he murmured, still unsure if his words were coming out.

He tried to reach for her, but felt himself falling, followed by some shouting, and then everything went black.

## MOIRA

"He's lost a lot of blood." Moira's hands trembled as she followed behind the men.

Emma had issued orders for clean linens and boiled water and Shona had run off to get her various herbs, ointments and a kit for sewing wounds.

"We'll get him patched up," Ewan murmured. "With ye and Shona here taking care of him, he'll be right as rain afore ye know it."

Moira nodded, though her gaze was on the stairs in front of her and the trail of blood dripping from Rory's fingertips. The MacDonald's, ruthless bastards that they were, had torn him to shreds with their blades. Anger and fear made her eyes tear, but she knew she couldn't shed a single one. Not if she was going to be able to concentrate on the care of his injuries.

The men took Rory to the chamber he shared with her, and she regretted every moment she'd resisted reuniting with him. They could have spent the last few days making love, telling each other how much they loved one another, instead of her trying to figure out ways to avoid him.

Dammit, why was she so stubborn?

Deep down, she'd known all along he was the only man for her. That was why she never committed to Dickie. Rory was her one and only.

*I will love ye, forever, mo chridhe.*

His barely audible words rang loud and clear in her mind.

Logan laid Rory on the bed, cutting away his clothes with a blade, while a servant rolled him from one side to the other to remove the fabric completely and check for wounds on his back.

"A slice along his left rib, none other on the back," Logan stated.

A sheet was laid over his middle for dignity. Ribbons of red marked his shoulder, his arms, torso and legs. Ewan and Logan left to take stock of the damage below in the courtyard and the moors beyond. The wounded needed to be cared for and the dead needed to be buried.

Servants rushed from the chamber to see about the linens and boiled water.

With Rory settled on the bed, and the two of them alone momentarily, Moira slid her fingers across his brow, a tender moment, that only she would remember. "I will love ye forever, too."

Rory's fingers twitched and he whispered something, but she couldn't make it out.

"I'm going to heal ye, so I can tell ye when ye're awake how verra much I love ye." Moira blew out a jagged breath and pressed her lips together hard to cease their tremble. "No tears," she murmured. "Hold it together."

Shona returned in a swish of skirts and a no-nonsense attitude. "Emma will be along shortly. She said the excitement was a little too much and she needed to lie down."

"Of course," Moira murmured, watching her sister set out various ointments and herbs on the table.

"I'll make a poultice while ye clean his wounds," Shona said.

"Yes."

Several servants filed in with pots of boiling water and clean linens. One pot was put near the hearth, the fire stoked, and the other was poured into the washbasin for Moira to use. Taking a cloth, she dipped it into the hot water.

"Is there whisky?" Shona asked someone.

Moira could use a drink....

She rung out the linen, her fingers red from the heat of the water, and pressed the cloth to one wound and then the next, cleaning away the blood. The wounds still seeped, and the water in the basin was thick with red. A servant dumped it out the window and gave her a fresh round of water for her to continue. She was methodical in her cleaning, and as she went, Shona dripped whisky on the wounds and then packed each with a clove-scented salve. They both worked to sew the cuts, mostly in silence, and Moira was pleased to see that only a few were truly deep, the rest mostly superficial.

Rory woke once, when they worked to sew up the deepest of cuts. He lashed out at them, catching Moira on her shoulder, enough that she was knocked off balance and fell.

"Are ye all right?" Shona called, pinning him down with the help of two waiting servants. Shona poured a healthy dose of some foul smelling tincture down his throat.

"I'm fine." Moira swallowed away her tears and returned to his bedside.

"We'll hold him while the tincture sets in, you sew."

The tincture didn't take long, his breathing became long and slow, slightly labored, and he no longer lashed out. After his wounds were sewn, poultices were pressed to each and they worked to wrap his injuries in thick linen bandages. By the time they were done he looked like a mummy. Linen coiled around his arms, his torso, his legs, and his head.

"I pray he heals quick," Moira said.

"He's a strong man." Shona smiled, and then whispered, "Willing to cross the bounds of time to fetch ye."

Moira glanced at her sister. "How do ye do it? How do ye manage? Because more than anything, I want to stay with him, but I'm afraid."

"Ye no longer wish to go home?"

Moira reached out to touch a part of skin on his arm that wasn't covered. "Not if I can't bring him and ye with me."

Shona reached over Rory's body to grab Moira's hand. "It's quite a lot easier than ye'd think. When ye are happy, it does not matter what time ye're in. I've found a purpose here. I can help so many more people here with my skills than I ever could back home."

"Then I can, too."

"Yes. But ye would most likely be doing so at your own castle."

"My own?" Moira raised a brow.

"Did ye not realize? If Rory is laird of his clan, he'll have to go to his own castle, and if ye decide to go with him, to become his wife, ye'll be the lady of the castle."

"Wow." That was a lot to swallow. "I'd never thought of that."

Shona laughed. "Well, ye've got some time, I think. Do ye want to rest, and I can watch over him for a little while?"

Moira shook her head. "Thank ye, but no. I want to stay with him."

"All right, then I shall go and help tend the wounded below. Let me know if ye need more help. And if he starts to catch a fever, have a servant fetch me. I've a tea that I made with coriander, willow bark, chamomile and a touch of hemlock that should help reduce it."

If it were anyone else offering hemlock to the man she loved, Moira might be suspicious, but she knew Shona had the intelligence to use the right amount.

Moira pulled her sister into an embrace, feeling the closeness once more that they'd had for so many years. For so long it had only been them. Now they each had someone else to add to their little family. "Thank ye."

"Ye would do the same for me."

"I would. I missed ye so much."

"I missed ye, too." Shona stroked Moira's hair. "He's going to live."

Moira's throat was thick with emotion. "I pray it's so."

"I know it. Ewan suffered injuries much like this, and he, too, survived. They are strong men. Built to withstand battle."

"Like gods in the arena."

"Exactly."

In her sister's arms, Moira finally let fall the tears she'd been holding back.

## SHONA

SHONA PRESSED HER HAND TO HER STOMACH IN THE corridor outside of Rory and Moira's chamber. She'd been fighting nausea for the last hour. Grasping at the wall for balance, she dragged in some steady breaths and made her way, slow step after slow step, to her own chamber that she shared with Ewan.

As soon as the door was shut, she rushed to the washbasin and unloaded the contents of her stomach.

Dear heavens, she hoped she wasn't getting sick. There was no time for that. There were many wounded that she needed to help tend.

Again, she pressed her hand to her belly, feeling a small knot that hadn't been there before. Small, but noticeable. Was it possible? Had the magic of the stone glen worked? Was she with child?

And how far along? If she'd conceived that night, then she could be almost three months along, even though only a few days had passed.

She swished out her mouth with the minty water she kept beside the basin, and then sank to the floor, trembling. An uncontrollable half-laugh, half-sob escaped her just as Ewan entered.

"What's wrong?" He dropped to his knees beside her. "Is it Rory? Was it worse than we thought?"

Ewan gathered her in his arms, and she gripped onto his shirt and kissed his face. "Nothing like that. Nothing bad at all. What are ye doing here? Are ye not tending the wounded and dead?"

"There are many helping. I came to check on ye."

"I'm wonderful." Her voice held a quality of joy that startled him, for he pulled back to stare at her. "Though I do feel a little guilty about saying that considering..."

"What is it? Tell me!"

She could hold back no longer. "I think I'm with child. I think the magic worked."

Ewan fell back on his behind, staring dazed at her middle. "Truly?"

"Aye. Feel it." She grabbed his hand and placed it over the small knot. "Can ye feel the difference?"

He nodded. "I want to see it. Take off your clothes."

Shona laughed and climbed to her feet, stripping off her gown and chemise. Sure enough, when she looked down, there was a slight swell.

Ewan got up on his knees and scooted closer, his hands gripping her hips. He stared at her belly for a long time, and then kissed it, murmuring, "Our bairn. Life we created."

Shona ran her fingers through his hair. "Ours."

"Och, love." Ewan stood and scooped her up. "Let me worship ye."

"Ye already do."

He chuckled and carried her to the bed. "On this day with so much death, so much strife, I've just found out the happiest news. I'm going to make love to ye, Shona."

She sighed, reaching for him. "Then get over here and do it."

## RORY

RORY WAS DREAMING. HE MUST BE.

But it was the strangest thing.

He was running through the snow. It was cold. There was a little lad racing beside him, beaming smiles. Laughter sounded from behind. When he turned to look, there was a fading shadow. A figure of a woman, and she was calling to him. Where she stood, the oddest thing, there was no snow. It was sunny. He was drawn to her. He told the lad to come with him, but the lad shook his head. Rory didn't know which way to go. He felt the pull of the woman's call, and yet the lad was urging him forward, into the deepest part of the snow.

"Rory..." She called to him in a singsong voice that left him feeling the heat of her on his skin.

He shivered. He didn't want to be cold. Looking down, he saw he wasn't even dressed for the snow. He argued with the lad, but he ran off, laughing and singing.

Then she touched him. Stroked his head. Her face was a blur. But he could sense who she was. "Moira," he said. "How did ye get here?"

"Ye brought me, love."

"Oh, right..."

"Drink this..."

The sunny meadow disappeared, and he felt himself being dragged into a tunnel. His head started to pound, his body ached, and dizziness made him nauseous. He was trembling. Sweating.

"What's happening?" he asked.

"Shh... Ye'll be all right. Drink."

Rory didn't want to drink. He was already feeling sick to his stomach. And so dizzy.

Liquid pooled in his mouth. But he hadn't parted his lips. How did she get him to drink?

"That's good," she said, encouraging.

"Vile," he croaked after swallowing.

She giggled. "Yes, but it will take away the pain. Ye need to rest. To heal."

And then she was brushing her lips over his, and he smiled. "Ye're here to stay?" he whispered.

"Yes. I'm here to stay."

He sank back into the meadow.

Some time later, he woke once more, throbbing in pain all over his body. He blinked his eyes open to see Moira lying on the bed beside him. She was asleep. So beautiful and peaceful.

"I love ye," he said to her.

She opened her eyes, a smile on her face and reached over

to touch his forehead. "Your fever is breaking. That's a good sign."

"I want ye to marry me." He was determined to tell her before he fell back into the dark; he needed to know that she wanted to be with him. When he'd been out on that battlefield, not knowing what would happen between the two of them had been his only regret.

"Yes, Rory. I'll marry ye." She leaned up on her elbow and pressed a gentle kiss to his lips.

"Good. Verra good." He smiled, stroked her face and twirled a lock of her hair around his finger.

"Where is my son?" he asked, feeling the darkness sweeping over him again.

"He is safe, locked in a tower chamber. He's a guest Logan said." Moira chewed her lip. "Ranulf curses your name from morning until night."

Rory laughed. "As would I."

"Ye're a good man, Rory MacLeod. One day he will see that. Ye did not have to save his life. But ye did."

"I am his father. I swore to protect him the day he was born, and I fell through on that duty once already."

"Do not blame yourself." She stroked his cheek. "In time he will understand."

"I canna live without ye, Moira. Dinna leave me."

"I'm not going anywhere." She cuddled up as close as she could to him without touching his wounds.

"I am the very luckiest man in all of time."

# EPILOGUE

*Two months later...*

"We're finally home." Moira beamed at her new husband, seated behind her, as they rode through the gates of Dunleod Castle.

"Aye, love. Finally." Rory pressed a kiss to the top of her head.

"This is *my* home," Ranulf grumbled.

Behind them, Ranulf was seated on his own horse, though his hands were tied at the wrists and he had two guards flanking him so he couldn't escape or try to hurt anyone. He was still bent on killing Rory, but he said so less and less often, which the two of them took as a good sign that his hatred was ebbing. With every chance he got, Rory showed the lad kindness, and Moira found out all of his favorite foods and had them taken to his tower chamber. Logan had taken the lad out to the fields and Ewan had trained with him so his body didn't shrivel to nothing. Overall, for a man who threatened bodily harm or death to everyone he saw, Ranulf was treated pretty darn well.

"Dinna let him spoil our homecoming," Rory whispered. His arms tightened around her middle. "The people will be kind to ye."

"Why should they? Are we not considered usurpers?" She said it quiet enough that no one could hear her.

Rory's chin scraped the top of her head as he shook it. "Nay, love. They've known me since I was a bairn, and they know how much the old laird respected me. I had a letter from the clan elders while I was recovering, declaring their full support."

"And what of Ranulf?"

"He is my son. My first-born. He shall inherit."

Moira patted his arm and glanced up behind her. "That is exactly as it should be."

The people of the clan gathered at the gates, shouting their welcome, the children tossing fresh spring flowers, one little girl coming forward with a crown of gillyflowers which Moira gratefully took and placed on her head. The little girl beamed excitement at seeing the lady of the castle wearing her creation.

As the days had continued to pass, the more she had become used to the sixteenth century. The thought of returning to present day rarely touched her mind, and never without her loved ones. She was going to be an auntie soon. When they'd left Castle Gealach, Shona had been about six months pregnant.

Rory reined in his mount, and dismounted from behind her, reaching up to take her down. She placed her hands on his shoulders and slid from the saddle, her legs weary from their journey to Skye.

"My laird, my lady," an elder looking man with kind eyes approached.

"Tomas." Rory's smile widened. He obviously new this man. "Allow me to introduce my wife, Lady Moira MacLeod, formerly Moira Wallace of Edinburgh."

She smiled, a secret, knowing smile. They'd concocted the story of her birth, keeping the place she'd loved and called home, as well as tying her to the Bruce through Wallace, a reminder that she had Ayreshire blood running through her veins. But never would they admit that, in case MacDonald caught wind of it.

Tomas bowed before her, as did the rest of the clan. "We humbly pledge our loyalty and our lives to ye both."

Each and every person present shouted the same and Moira felt such a huge weight lift from her shoulders. They were accepted. They were welcomed. She could not have asked for anything more.

"We thank ye for the warm welcome! We shall celebrate tonight! But for now, we've had a long journey and your mistress and I wish to rest." Rory looked down at her and winked.

"We've a room prepared. The rider ye sent ahead gave us your instructions on how to prepare it."

Moira raised a brow and Rory winked at her in return.

"Excellent. My thanks for seeing it done," Rory said to Tomas.

They'd been married before leaving Castle Gealach, when Rory had finally healed, but they'd left in such a hurry, there'd not been time to actually consummate their marriage. Both of them were itching to get upstairs and close the door.

Rory swept her up, and she wrapped her arms around his neck. "I shall walk ye across our threshold."

"I will allow it," she teased.

"Ye're a bossy wench."

"I'm glad ye remembered."

Rory jogged up the few stairs to the castle, sweeping

through the entrance. Ahead of them was an arched door to the great hall and to the right of it was another leading to circular stairs. Rory took the steps two at a time until reaching the third floor. He didn't stop until he was entering a chamber that smelled of sweet flowers and herbal spice.

"Oh my," Moira breathed.

The entire room had been filled with blooms in vases and herb-scented candles, lit to glowing. 'Twas beautiful and romantic.

"We've not yet had a honeymoon, so I thought it best to give ye a small one here."

"This is beautiful." She pressed her mouth to his, savoring his scent and taste and the fact that she could actually do this. Have him in her arms. In her life. "Thank ye so much."

"Ye need never thank me for treating ye the way I should."

"But I will all the same, Rory. I've been to the other side, and I know how good I have it."

He chuckled. "Love, I am the one thanking ye, every blessed day."

He carried her to their bed, and laid her gently upon it. "Shall I get ye a glass of wine?"

Though she would have loved one any other time, she shook her head. "My only thirst is to feel your body on mine. It has been entirely too long."

"More than five hundred years," he teased.

She giggled. "My point exactly."

"Then I'd best help ye to undress, because if I dinna feel my skin on yours, I just might go mad."

She felt the very same way. Rory slid his fingers over her collarbones, and then to the center of her chest, untying the ribbons of her bodice and then the front of her chemise, baring her breasts to the scented air of their room. But she didn't feel exposed, if anything, the hungry look in his eyes only made her body come more alive. Her nipples grew taut, and she sucked in a breath as he skimmed his palms over her flesh.

"Good god, your breasts are even better than I remembered." He leaned forward, nuzzling the surface of each before breathing hotly on one taut peek. He slid his tongue around the edges of her nipple, teasing her, taunting her, making her gasp with need, but not quite satisfying her with what she really wanted. Instead of drawing one into his mouth to suck, he stood. "I need to get undressed."

She groaned, but smiled at the same time. Rory only laughed.

"If there is one thing we've taught each other, it is that to tease only makes the pleasure all the more delicious," he imparted.

That was definitely the truth.

So while he worked to remove his clothing, she climbed from the bed, sliding her fingers over his arms, his chest, and caressing the muscles that covered his ribs around to his back. She followed the trail of her hands, standing behind him and kissing his spine. His skin was smooth and rippled with strength.

Moira skimmed her lips across his back, nipping at his shoulder blade, relishing his quick, indrawn breath. He'd stilled when she stood, having not moved as she touched him, his kilt still in place.

"Are ye not going to remove this?" she asked, tugging his belt.

"Och, lass, but I can barely recall my own name when ye touch me."

"Let me do it then." She stepped in front of him, gripping his belt and yanking until it was unclasped and the fabric of his kilt fell to the floor at their feet. "That's better," she murmured, leaning forward to press a kiss against his skin, his heart pounding beneath her lips.

Her gaze was drawn down to the thickness of his erection that curved upward toward her. She slid her fingers beneath him, running them up the length of his thick cock, feeling him shiver, goose bumps rising on the skin of his arms.

"Now, I'm wearing too many clothes," she mused.

"Aye. Let me help he with that." His eyes were hooded, his grin wicked.

Moira loved that look. The gaze that said he was going to do incredible things to her body.

Nimble fingers removed the rest of her clothes. Velvet tongue skimmed over her heated skin. Teasing teeth scraped over sensitive flesh. Hard body glided up the length of hers. Touching. Tantalizing. Tempting.

Rory was not the only one who could play such games. As she devoured his mouth with her own, Moira massaged the muscles of his chest, rubbed her breasts against his skin, lifted her leg around his hip and ground her wet sex against the rigid length of his shaft until he, too, was panting and groaning with the need to bury himself inside her.

He threaded his fingers in her hair, yanked her head, gentle enough not to hurt, forceful enough to make her moan. His mouth scraped deliciously over the column of her throat, then her chin where he playfully bit her, and finally to her mouth where he claimed her as his own.

With swift possessiveness he thrust his tongue between her parted lips, tangled against hers. Tasted. Taunted. Took.

"Ye're mine," he growled.

"Yes," she sighed.

"Forever."

"And ever."

Rory lifted her in the air and she wrapped her legs around his hips, her slick folds sliding over his unyielding cock, making her legs tremble. Frissons of heated desire and hunger raced through her veins.

"I want ye inside me," she murmured against his mouth. "Now."

"Love, ye have no idea." He gripped her beneath her thighs, shifting her so she could feel the head of his cock at her entrance.

Moira deepened their kiss, wanting to own his mouth as much as he owned hers.

Rory laid her on the bed, kissing his way down to her breasts, flicking his tongue over one nipple and then the other. She gripped his hair, tugging, arching her back to get closer, yanking so that he would suck harder.

"And this, ye remember this?" He reached for a vial on the nightstand beside the bed.

"What is it?"

His grin widened. "A medieval version of what ye love."

"Ye're the medieval version of what I love," she giggled.

Rory bit the cork, yanking it free and the scent of mint wafted toward her.

"Oh," she sighed. "I do love that."

He dripped a few drops onto one nipple, slowly rubbing the minty oil over her skin until she tingled. All over she trembled. Between her thighs was soaked with need. But still he took his time.

Rory loomed over her, bending low to graze his tongue over her nipple again, this time the coolness of the mint contrasted with the heat of his tongue and she gasped, not having felt such sensations since the last time she'd been with him. As he toyed with her breasts, he caressed his way down her body to between her thighs, bringing the cool-heat with him as he rubbed the oil over her clit.

She tilted her hips, all but begging him to enter inside her.

"Not so fast," he murmured.

And then he was scooting down, licking a path from her breasts to her navel and lower. Her knees fell open, wider, her sex, cold, and hot, at the same time. She quivered, eyes wide as she watched him, and he watched her.

"Ye know ye want this."

"Oh, yes, please."

He breathed hotly over her clit, not quite touching, enough that she groaned in both frustration and pleasure. She reached down to grab hold of his hair.

"Nay, love..."

"Then let me pleasure ye at the same time."

Rory's grin widened. He flopped onto his back and tugged her over him. She readily straddled his face, her mouth falling just inches from his cock.

He massaged her arse, the backs of her thighs, and he parted her folds before diving forward, his tongue like soft fire lapping at her clit.

"Ohmygod..." She'd always loved the feel of his mouth on her, but there was something infinitely different in knowing that he was hers forever.

She reached for the minty vial, pouring a drop into her hand, and spilling more as she could barely concentrate on anything other than the intense pleasure scorching between her thighs.

Her head dropped to his hipbone, and she kissed him there, working her way back to his cock while her hand massaged the cool oil over his turgid flesh. Rory groaned his pleasure, a sound she mimicked against his skin as she took him deep into her mouth.

The medieval oil tasted better than the modern version. Non-synthetic. It was actually pretty good. She licked around the head of his cock, up and down the length of him, and then sucked him deep, bobbing her head in time with the pump of his hips.

Not three sucks later, she was caught off guard by the orgasm that ripped through her body, making her clamp her thighs against his head, and moan deeply against his cock still buried near the back of her throat.

"*Mo chreach*," Rory cursed, grabbing her by the hair and pulling her off him. "I dinna want to finish yet."

He was flipping her onto her back once more, his thick, hard body looming above her, his thighs spreading hers.

"God, I missed ye," he said, capturing her mouth once more for a searing kiss.

Moira wrapped her arms around his shoulders, clinging to him, her legs pinned around his hips. The head of his cock probed against her still quivering entrance, and then he was surging forward, burying himself deep inside her. Filling. Stretching. Owning.

Both of them cried out, the sounds of their pleasure echoing from stone wall to stone wall. Hands stroked. Tongues tasted. Lips locked.

He thrust inside her, ground his pelvis to hers, arched up, and slowly withdrew. A pattern that changed the closer she came to climaxing, until she felt for certain he was tormenting her on purpose.

She listened intently to his breathing, to the sounds of his moans, cries of her own pleasure, relishing gasps. His groans grew deeper, guttural, primal. He pumped harder, hastening his pace. Plunging deep. Tiny tremors quickened inside her. So close.

She dug her nails into his back, gasping with ecstasy. Rory's forehead fell to the crook of her shoulder, his tongue flicking out to taste a drop of her sweat.

And then they were both coming, both of them crying out, shuddering, riding the waves of boundless pleasure.

"I never—" Rory gulped, his breathing as erratic as the pounding of her heart. "Before I met ye, I never thought I'd be this happy." He fell to the side, pulling her into his arms. "Never thought I'd find love. Never thought I'd find such pleasure. And I... I could go another round... Saints, but ye have undone me."

"Nay, I have made ye whole, just as ye have completed me." She walked her fingers along the sinew of his chest.

Rory chuckled, and hugged her tighter, pressing a tender kiss to her lips. "Aye, and we just proved together we can make one."

Moira laughed with him, but their laughs were soon quelled by more kisses, and proving just how much they could be one again.

❧❧❧

While this may be *The End* for now—'tis not truly over...
Look for the next installments of the Highland Bound series:

*Highlander Undone*
*Highlander Unraveled*
*Draped in Plaid* — *March 23, 2021*

WANT MORE SEXY TIME-TRAVELING HIGHLANDERS? CHECK out my Touchstone novella series!

*Highland Steam*
*Highland Brawn*
*Highland Tryst*
*Highland Heat*

*If you enjoyed* **HIGHLANDER UNDONE**, *please spread the word by leaving a review on the site where you purchased your copy,* *or a reader site such as Goodreads! I love to hear from readers! Visit me on Facebook:* https://www.facebook.com/elizaknightfiction. I'm also on Instagram @ElizaKnightFiction and Twitter: @ElizaKnight *Many thanks!*

**Stay tuned for Summer 2021 and Eliza's brand new Scottish Regency series — SCOTS OF HONOR!**

Highland war heroes rebuilding their lives grapple with ladies forging their own paths—who will win?

Regency Scotland comes alive in the vibrant and sexy new SCOTS OF HONOR series by USA Today bestselling author Eliza Knight. Scottish military heroes, who want nothing more than to lay low after the ravages of war in 19th century France, find their Highland homecomings vastly contradict their simple desires. Especially when they meet the feisty lasses who are tenacious enough to take them on, and show them just what they've been missing out of life. In battle they can't be beaten, but in love, they all find the ultimate surrender.

*Return of the Scot*
*The Scot is Hers*
*Taming the Scot*

WANT TO READ MORE SCOTTISH ROMANCE NOVELS BY ELIZA? CHECK OUT HER STOLEN BRIDE SERIES!

*The Highlander's Temptation*
*The Highlander's Reward*

*The Highlander's Conquest*
*The Highlander's Lady*
*The Highlander's Warrior Bride*
*The Highlander's Triumph*
*The Highlander's Sin*
*Wild Highland Mistletoe (a Stolen Bride winter novella)*
*The Highlander's Charm (a Stolen Bride novella)*
*A Kilted Christmas Wish – a contemporary Holiday spin-off*
*The Highlander's Surrender*
*The Highlander's Dare*

## ABOUT THE AUTHOR

Eliza Knight is an award-winning and *USA Today* bestselling author of over fifty sizzling historical romance and erotic romance. Under the name E. Knight, she pens rip-your-heart-out historical fiction. While not reading, writing or researching for her latest book, she chases after her three children. In her spare time (if there is such a thing...) she likes daydreaming, wine-tasting, traveling, hiking, staring at the stars, watching movies, shopping and visiting with family and friends. She lives atop a small mountain with her own knight in shining armor, three princesses and two very naughty puppies. Visit Eliza at http://www.elizaknight.com or her historical blog History Undressed: www.historyundressed.com. Sign up for her newsletter to get news about books, events, contests and sneak peaks! http://eepurl.com/CSFFD

facebook.com/elizaknightfiction

twitter.com/elizaknight

instagram.com/elizaknightfiction

bookbub.com/authors/eliza-knight

goodreads.com/elizaknight

Made in the USA
Monee, IL
10 April 2021